GW01366949

THAT SPLIT ETERNAL SECOND

Anthony Partridge

MINERVA PRESS
MONTREUX LONDON WASHINGTON

THAT SPLIT ETERNAL SECOND
Copyright © Anthony Partridge 1995

All Rights Reserved

No part of this book may be reproduced in any form,
by photocopying or by any electronic or mechanical means,
including information storage or retrieval systems,
without permission in writing from both the copyright owner
and the publisher of this book.

ISBN 1 85863 589 6

First Published 1995 by
MINERVA PRESS
1 Cromwell Place,
London SW7 2JE

Printed in Great Britain by
B.W.D. Ltd., Northolt, Middlesex

THAT SPLIT ETERNAL SECOND

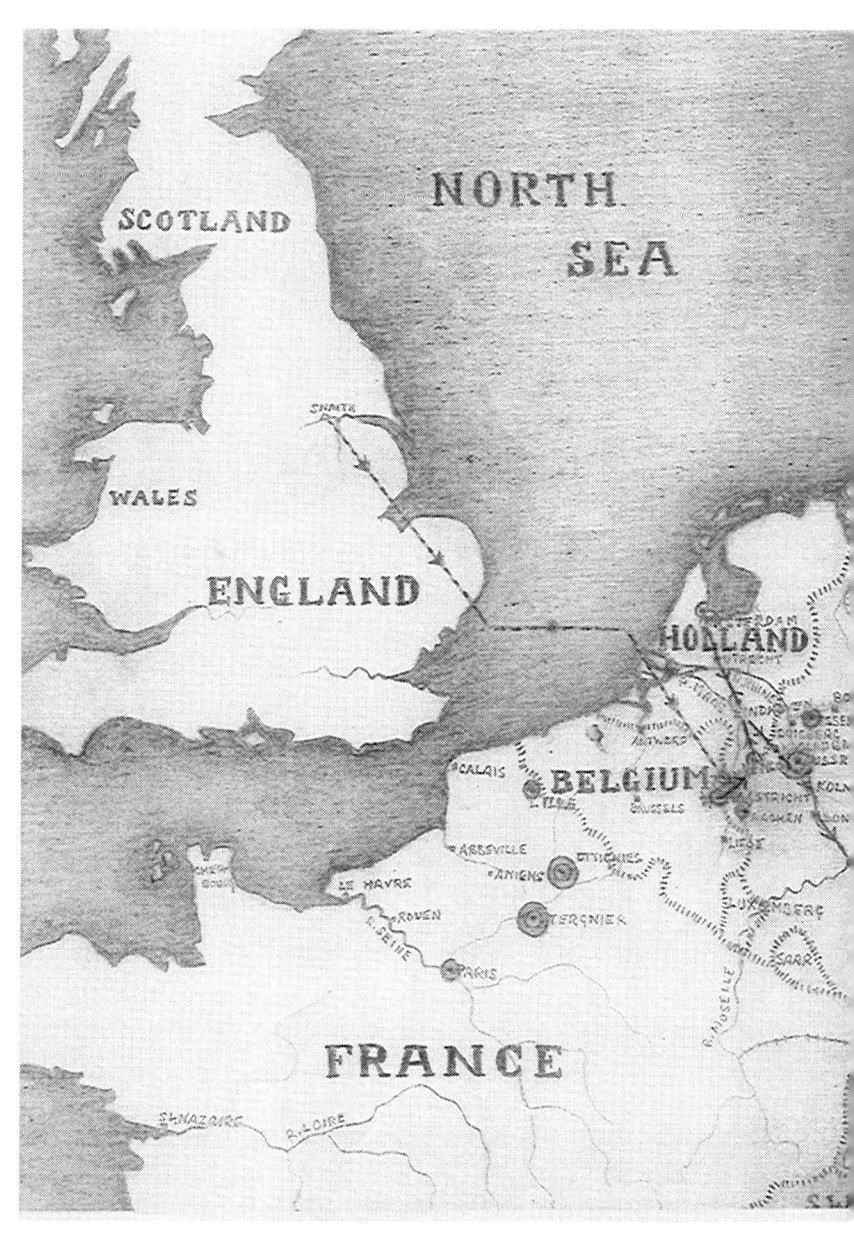

Map of Europe drawn by author in crayon, whilst in POW camp.

(cont.) Each ring around the German cities denotes a bombing raid, and the arrows, his travels as a POW.

Photograph of Author in uniform, 1942

"That Split Eternal Second"

White shafts of light that grope from far below
Accusing fingers from another world
Of darkness far beneath, and yet we know
They must not find us yet.

Mad bursts of orange flame that creep and claw
The blackened heights for us who vainly twist
And closer now until above the roar
Of motors comes the 'flak'.

We stiffen at the last unearthly sound
Of tearing fingers at the fuselage
That split eternal second . . .

Anon

*

How Long, O Lord, How Long?

I see your face (this now in dim relief)
Eyes fixed on nearing death with disbelief.
With drying lips I see you frame that cry
"O God! thy hand, for here I come to die"

How long have we to live, we cannot tell
And if we could we would not wish
So grim a secret to unfold itself
For puny hope remains until the end.

That date that we have made two days ahead
Will I, unmaimed and living still,
Be there to laugh and joke with you
As we have done so many times before?

Oh useless thought, and yet I see once more
The face I loved that laughed and said
"So long old boy, please keep my breakfast warm"
And never did return, but plunged instead
From moonlit heights, in seething mass of flame.

Today we live but then this coming night
May find us trapped beneath the waves
In riddled turret - silent - all alone
With sightless eyes fixed on forgotten foe.

When landing safe, alive to go again
We gently lift those huddled men
Whose lives departed high above the clouds
We wonder why they died - and we still live.

Anon

*

About the Author

Anthony Partridge was educated at Merchant Taylors' School, and in 1937 he left hoping to join the R.A.F., but shortly afterwards suffered a serious motorbike accident which put him in and out of hospital for the next three years.

He was finally able to join the R.A.F., where, as he puts it, 'as long as you could see and hear and were keen, you were in!' Training as a pilot in the Southern States of America, he was then remustered to train as a bomb-aimer in Canada, when the urgent call came for other trades to make up crews for the increasing number of bombers required. Joining 51 Squadron Snaith in 1943 during the Battle of Berlin, possibly the worst period of the R.A.F. losses of the war, he recalls the hopes and fears of the time.

The graphic accounts of life on an operational squadron taken from drawings and notes at the time give an insight into those exhilarating and dangerous days.

Having almost completed a tour of operations, he was shot down over Holland, and became one of the lucky ones to escape a burning aircraft to become a prisoner of war. In great detail, he is able to recount the ups and downs of P.O.W. life, the harassment of the German Authorities, the amusing exploits, and the reprisals that were to follow. Later he, with two others, escaped from a marching column, to endure some tense moments while living off the land, in an attempt to reach the Allied lines, just a fortnight before the end of the war.

The author, now a retired landscape gardener, lives in a small village in the heart of Dorset, and has a wife and two daughters.

To The Many Who Did Not Return

Acknowledgements

I am deeply indebted to my cousin, Haddon Partridge, who with great patience committed my handwriting into typescript, and to my brother-in-law, Derek Truscott, for presenting me on the occasion of my 70th birthday with the Bomber Command War Diaries, which brought back so many memories.

My daughter Stella has given me invaluable practical assistance, and special thanks are due to her and to my wife Margaret and daughter Clare, without whose help and encouragement this story would not have been written.

Chapter 1

We had set course from Mablethorpe just before dusk. Below, in the fading light, the tide was going out, revealing the miles of mud flats and the little streams and rivulets escaping from the pent up dykes which drained the marshes.

The sea took on a leaden sheen, broken only by the lonely trails of the little coasters and fishing boats going home. In the air we were not alone.

Aircraft were to be seen on all sides struggling for height, while occasional splashes far below denoted bombers jettisoning their loads and returning home with engine trouble.

It had been a long anxious day. During the morning we had learnt that 'operations' were on and we had checked our aircraft with the ground crew and seen the overload fuel tanks - it was going to be a long trip. They were on their trolleys being delivered to the aircraft which were dispersed on round oily 'pans' under the trees, surrounded by the ground crews, who were already starting to crank up the tanks into the bomb-bays and connect up the fuel lines. The Halifax had a limited range, but with this additional fuel was able to reach practically the whole of Germany.

The majority of our crew had now been flying together for nearly a year, through operational training at Harwell, where we carried out all our practice bombing on Wellingtons, to Heavy Conversion Unit, dealing with four engined bombers. We were all sergeants, Lewis Rothwell, the pilot whom we called Lewie or Skipper came from Manchester, 'Nobby' Clark, the navigator from Bayswater, and myself the bomb-aimer. Then there were Ted Boyles, the engineer from Newton Abbot, and 'Mac' McQuater, the wireless operator from Ayrshire. The two gunners were 'Rebel' Sinclair, mid-upper gunner from Canada, and John McGlynn, the tail gunner from Middlesborough, whose granny kept a fish and chip shop. He was only nineteen and had been in the R.A.F. just a year.

One might say a motley crew, but we were mates. We lived together, drank together and flew together and were rarely separated, to the extent that we knew each other's strengths and weaknesses. We were indeed fortunate that throughout our operating life our crew was never broken up until one devastating trip when Ted was carried wounded from the aircraft. This was to be our first operation. The C.O. had told us on arrival at 51 Squadron SNAITH, that we would be given time to settle in with one or two easy 'trips', but 'Bomber Harris' had decreed otherwise, and the station was now cut off from the outside world.

We wandered over to 'Briefing' with some apprehension and sat down with what appeared to be the whole squadron. The Nissen hut was packed as the C.O. came in and we all stood up and waited for the wave of his hand from the stage. The huge map was uncovered and there it was - Berlin, the outward and return courses marked out with thick black tape, the danger spots of known gun concentrations and fighter aerodromes marked in red.

"This is a maximum effort," announced the C.O. "Upwards of a thousand aircraft in two waves will be taking part and 'Pathfinders' will be marking a western segment of the city with 'Wanganui' sky markers, two minutes before arrival of the first wave. There will be a following wind over the target area, so you should be able to rattle through. Synchronise watches!" 'Wanganui' we knew was used in cloud conditions and consisted of various coloured sky markers suspended on parachutes to mark the aiming point. We had seen these demonstrated up in the Yorkshire moors some weeks before.

The briefing continued with details of navigational aids available, fuel loads and type of bombs.

We would be carrying a block-buster, rather like an old fashioned pillar-box only bigger, with incendiaries in the wing bays. Finally the weather report claimed that it was clear for take-off with increasing high cloud over Germany, which would help to obscure the moon, and over the target area, the possibility of low cloud.

The Met officer was able to predict the likely conditions by the weather report from the special Meteorological Unit Spitfire, taken during the early morning. These Spitfires were painted duck-egg blue, were highly polished and carried no armament, only a series of cameras and instruments.

Dismissed from the briefing room, Nobby and I visited the WAAFs in the map-room (we were to make many visits to the map-room) and came away with a selection of all, or any maps which might be of value should the weather remain clear and the moon remain visible. One never knew.

As take-off was early - it was to be a long trip - we all strolled down to the mess for our flying supper, bacon and eggs and almost anything else one could wish for.

We ate well, though it was an unusually subdued meal, our thoughts almost entirely on the task ahead. It would be more than eight hours before we ate again, apart from the issue of barley-sugars handed out on departure.

And now the moment had come, and we were glad. Into the locker rooms, empty the pockets, and on with the gear, flying helmets with oxygen masks attached, a succession of flying suits with large woollies of all descriptions and then the padded flying boots and finally the parachute harness.

We were ready, with uncertain laughter, tinged with bravado and apprehension. Having collected our parachutes and individual dinghy packs from the parachute section, all crews clambered aboard the transports which were to take us to our dispersals almost a mile away. Although of course we had flown our 'Halibag' M H-A all over England on night 'cross countries', this was to be our first test under fire, but as the number of our 'operations' mounted we were to become inordinately fond of our aircraft which was to bring us safely home so many times.

A last chat with the ground crew, amid exhortations to 'blast the bastards' we clambered aboard having taken the final precautions of anointing one of the huge tyres before re-adjusting our cumbersome flying gear.

On principle we never used the Elsan in the rear of the aircraft, a fact not unappreciated by the ground crew.

Just before starting up, a strange ritual took place. This at first caused some amusement, but immediate realisation of its earnestness was evident, and later we would not have flown without first witnessing it.

The youngest 'erk' (the lowest form of life in the R.A.F.) ran along the front of the aircraft, kissing his hand and leaping up to slap each huge engine cowling in turn. We were impressed and settled into our positions in cheerful mood.

"Start engines," shouted the Skipper, leaning out of the cockpit window, and the ground crew connected up the battery trolley below. "Port outer-Port inner," and with a thumbs up from the 'Chiefy' on the ground, each engine in turn rattled and coughed into life, spewing great gouts of white then blue smoke as the huge double banked Bristol radials cleared.

With all four engines running evenly, each engine was run up separately, to check 'revs', magneto, oil and boost pressures on the dials in the cockpit and in the engineers 'office', where Ted was also responsible for changing fuel tanks as the flight progressed. At the 'chocks away' signal to 'Chiefy' and a boost to the outer engines for taxi-ing, we began to roll slowly out of the dispersal to join the procession of bombers passing down the taxi strip to wait at the end of the runway.

Taking our place in the queue, we were at once aware of the impressive sight these great bombers made, stretching away into the distance, nose to tail for perhaps half a mile. We felt in good company, and this was happening all over Yorkshire, Lincolnshire and East Anglia. As we prepared to turn on to the main runway Lewie called over the intercom, "Take off positions," and the crew settled into the centre well of the aircraft.

I was in the fortunate position of being able to click up a retractable seat over the steps down to the bombing well and sit in the co-pilot's seat to assist in the take-off as necessary. Waiting for the 'green', Lewie set fine pitch to the propellors and 10% flap for take-off.

The green signal flashed from the dome on the top of the control hut, and with brakes full on and full 'revs' we hovered for a moment, waiting for the surge. With a hiss as the brakes were released the aircraft seemed to leap forward, 'props' clawing at the still air and we were propelled down the runway.

With a full load of fuel and bombs, she did not want to 'unstick' but finally the rumble of the undercarriage ceased and we were airborne and climbing. As we gained height the vista below opened up and I thought how beautiful the countryside looked in the late afternoon sun. It was strange taking off on a night bombing raid in broad daylight, but we had a long way to go.

At 2000 feet we were able to see other bombers rising from their bases in close proximity, some so close in fact that their 'circuits' almost overlapped.

The whole of Yorkshire appeared to be one vast aerodrome. We felt strangely comforted amongst this great armada of aircraft, flying almost in a loose formation, but as darkness began to fall, they gradually disappeared and we were alone.

"Hello Skipper, Dutch coast coming up," I called over the intercom, "with heavy flak to the north."

"OK bomb-aimer, that will be the Frisians. Can you see the Zuider Zee?"

"'Fraid not Skipper, too much ground haze," I answered.

I was comfortably settled, lying on top of the escape hatch completely surrounded by glass - or rather perspex - back almost as far as my waist.

I had a wonderful view, up, down and sideways and by leaning over could just see the violet blue exhaust flames pouring from the exhaust stubs of the engines. Feeling very vulnerable, I arranged my dinghy pack on one side and clip-on parachute on the other to give some sense of protection. At least they would stop the odd bullet.

We had now plugged in our oxygen masks and were at the operating height of 17,000 feet. I had already set this on the bomb sight, together with aircraft speed and wind speed and direction as given at briefing. The machine would sort out all these figures and arrive at a happy medium.

Having checked the bomb release gear and the position of the release button on its short length of flex, I relaxed and enjoyed the fireworks ahead which were already impressive.

"Change of course, Skipper, alter course 075 degrees."

"OK navigator, 075 degrees it is. Keep a good look out everyone." This was all part of the feint set up at the briefing to encourage the enemy to think we were going for Hamburg.

Suddenly A-Able dropped alarmingly, shuddered until the bombs rattled, and returned to an even keel.

"No cause for alarm, probably a 'Halibag' up front," from the Skipper. Although sudden and unnerving, we were to become accustomed to the quite frequent effects of 'buffeting' when caught in the slipstream of bombers immediately and close in front. It helped to remind us that we were not alone. The moon had now risen as predicted and the high cloud above formed a huge white sheet, against which I could see a large gaggle of Lancasters, probably a 1000 feet above us. The Lancaster had a higher 'ceiling' than the Halifax, and we were always to be first in the queue for the night fighters. The respective losses of the two types of aircraft possibly reflected this.

A blinding orange light seared my eyes as from just in front a bomber slowly fell away, lit all the way to the ground in a cloud of burning fuel, to explode on impact in a shimmering cross of blazing light.

The Skipper called us up again on the intercom to remind us to keep a sharp look out for fighters. We did not need reminding. This was going to be a fighter night.

Leaving my position in the nose, I stood in the well beside the skipper and had a good look round, as attack was unlikely to come from dead ahead. Someone was catching it off to our port, and there was heavy flak and searchlights up ahead where other aircraft had obviously 'bought it'. I clambered through into Nobby's 'office', lifting the curtain and plugging in my oxygen to keep me going for a while, to inspect his spidery hieroglyphics. Some of us had done the prescribed course in navigation, but this was navigation under pressure, and I was glad it was not my department.

Nobby always seemed agitated and jumpy in the air, and although obviously highly strung, was totally efficient and never at a loss for a new course to fly, whatever the conditions. We had absolute confidence in him, and now that we were beyond the range of 'Gee', the radar beams directed from England, we relied upon him entirely. A-Able lurched suddenly and I rapidly returned to my horizontal position in the nose.

Heavy flak was now banging away under our port wing and Lewie eased her off to starboard a little. One never knew quite what to do for the best, as the enemy often seemed to fire in a diamond pattern. It was just luck.

"Time to alter course Skipper, 080 degrees target run."

"OK navigator. How far to target?" from the Skipper.

"About 50 miles, we should be on time."

Each leg of the trip was calculated on time and distance run, though any appreciable wind change could lead to a huge error in position. We were somewhat assured of our position from the frequent buffeting from our fellows in front and several bombers had passed close above and below during our change of course, their glowing exhaust stubs clearly visible.

The first wave of bombers was now approaching the target area and was being attacked with great force by the outer defences of Berlin.

Searchlights probed up through the gaps in the low cloud and there was a lot of muck up there in the sky. One hoped that enemy aircraft over England received the same warm reception.

A sudden shout brought us to action. "Corkscrew port, Skipper, Corkscrew port - fighter!" from Johnny in the rear turret. Lewie threw everything into one corner and A-Able dropped heavily to port and then heaved up into the first arc of the horizontal corkscrew to outwit the fighter. He was already firing, the long blue streaks of tracer passing above.

We hung on for dear life, flung about in all directions, having no warning of this violent escape manoeuvre. Nobby's instruments finished up in the front well and my carefully arranged parachute pack had gone. I would have to find it.

"All clear Skipper," from Rebel in the mid-upper turret.

"He's just gone over the top. After easier game, Messerschmitt 110."

"Thanks mid-upper, back onto course then," and Lewie eased the aircraft back on to an even keel.

It had been close, but we felt suddenly confident at having out flown one of their best night fighters. But we still had a long way to go, and already our eyes were aching from staring out into the unknown blackness.

The 'corkscrew' was probably the best evasive action against fighters. But it could be very dangerous from the point of view of other bombers in the stream, particularly if they happened to be carrying out the same action, as a large amount of airspace was required, with considerable loss of height.

The orange glow reflected in the sky ahead showed that the first wave were already bombing. Suddenly all hell was let loose. Heavy flak was all round us, above and below. The aircraft rocked and shuddered, bits rattled on the fuselage. Bright flashes blinded us, the noise above the roaring engines as we flew through the black smoke puffs and the aircraft was filled with the smell of the shell-bursts.

They were firing everything, and in this seemingly impenetrable barrage, how or why should we get through, when others were so unlucky? But nothing lasts for ever and we were soon out of accurate range and inspecting for damage.

"Pilot to crew, everyone all right?"

"OK Skipper," came the general reply.

"Ted, how are your instruments, engines and pressures OK?"

"Everything normal Skipper. I'll keep an eye on the fuel gauges though, in case we're losing any."

Nobby called, "Five minutes to zero hour," and I confirmed that we were dead on track. I then called up Nobby to check for any wind speed or direction changes to be made to the bomb-sight, glad that there were none, as things were becoming a bit hectic.

It was now like daylight. The moon above beat down on the high cloud and the searchlights lit up the undersides of the cloud below. I re-checked the bomb-sight and the release gear again. Everything must work first time - we could not go round again in this lot.

Clearly visible up ahead, the first wave of bombers was diving, weaving and corkscrewing in deadly earnest as Messerschmitt 109s and Focke Wulf 190s barrelled through the mass of bomber's, like fish in a goldfish bowl. It was an unearthly sight, but we were all too busy with our respective duties to dwell on it.

Nobby called, "Two minutes to Zero hour," as I looked down and marvelled at the pulsating orange glow reflected on the cloud below, and the red balls of flak rushing up to meet us. It did not seem to deter the night fighters.

Where were the new sky markers for our wave - were we too early, or had the pathfinder planes been shot down?

Nobby called, "New course 275 degrees on the way out, Skipper." I looked again through the bomb-sight above the flat slanting nose panel, the electrical bomb release knob to hand. As if by magic the shower of shimmering green sky markers appeared slightly off to our right, suspended on their parachutes, drifting slowly downwind amid the smoke.

"Bomb-doors open Skipper," I shouted.

"Bomb-doors open," he replied without a tremor and I switched on the bombing panel and photo-flash.

"Five degrees starboard," I called, waiting for the lumbering reaction of the Halifax to swing on to the markers.

Everything was happening at once, Lancasters and Halifaxes converged on the aiming point from all sides, jostling for position to line up with the markers and greatly increasing the chance of collision.

We were buffeted unmercifully. "Right. Steady-Right," I called with my nose on the bomb-sight.

It was impossible, the aircraft skidded about, rocked and shuddered in the slipstream of other bombers. Rebel called up from the mid-upper turret, "Lanc overhead Skipper, with bomb doors open." An added danger. We slid away, to start lining up again, the fighters having a picnic knowing that we were all now committed to our task.

"Left Left, Skipper, steady-steady," I called again as the markers jumped about in the tramlines of the bomb-sight. Only another few seconds and we would be away from this interminable straight and level flying.

I was suddenly reminded of the orders given at the briefing - undershooting causes 'creepback'. Some crews had been bombing early to escape from the maelstrom. "Right, steady-steady," I corrected as the markers slid down the tramlines and onto the cross wire, and I was glad to press the bomb tit, sensing the relief of the crew.

"Bombs going," and I watched the little lights clicking out in the control box. "Bombs gone - bomb doors shut," I called and A-Able seemed to leap upwards, suddenly relieved of her load, as the photo-flash went off far below.

'Taps full open' we prepared to flee the scene, although we still had several miles of 'day light' activity before clearing the outskirts of the city. And then once more into the friendly darkness and the hope of a boring flight home. I was now able to relax a little and scrambled back to check visually that all bombs had gone.

"Keep a good look out, chaps, we're not home yet," Lewie reminded us. "How's the fuel Ted? Everything OK?"

"OK Skipper, everything's fine."

We knew all was well. Any slight change of engine note would have immediately registered in our minds, and we were now prepared for the long haul to the channel and comparative safety.

Now acutely aware of the cold, those who could, moved about and changed position. There were so-called heating arrangements emanating from the engines but these were largely ineffective.

Above my head hung an obsolete Lewis gun and this I swore to have removed before we flew again. I was forever banging my head on this useless pea-shooter, and through the hole round its mounting, tore the most furious draught.

At last we were over the channel after an uneventful return trip, and with the I.F.F. (Identification Friend or Foe) switched on.

Ted now dispensed hot coffee from the huge flask we always carried. Lewie suggested that I take over for a bit while he had his coffee, and having put the aircraft on 'George', the automatic pilot, we changed places.

I unclicked 'George' and I was in charge. "Don't worry chaps, I won't attempt a 'corkscrew'!" I joked, refusing to listen to the spirited reply.

I had flown the Halifax occasionally, on night cross-countries and was still amazed at the time-lag on the controls, several seconds elapsing before anything definite happened, rather like flying a bus.

I had learnt to fly in the Southern States of America nearly two years earlier under the pilot training scheme, but was one of the unfortunates who were remustered to other trades half way through, following the end of the Battle of Britain and the new requirements for bomber crews.

Having returned to the cockpit, Lewie called Nobby and asked for an E.T.A. (Estimated Time of Arrival).

"About twenty minutes Skipper. We should cross the coast somewhere near Flamborough Head."

"Let me know if you can pinpoint anything bomb-aimer," and I replied that it was unlikely as we were descending into thin cloud and rain was already forming rivulets on the nose panels.

As E.T.A. approached and nothing was visible below, Lewie called up base and was given permission to join the circuit.

We descended through cloud, navigation lights on, to a minimum height above known high ground. At 2000 feet the cloud suddenly broke and there below us was the welcome sight of several flashing beacons giving their station call signs. Joining the circuit close to Snaith beacon, Lewie called up on R.T.

"Hallo Mable, Hallo Mable, A-Able, A-Able calling. Permission to pancake?"

Back came the reassuring voice, "Clear to pancake, A-Able pancake!"

Lowering the undercarriage and flaps Lewie turned into the final approach, the runway dimly outlined by the row of little winking lights.

I quickly regained my seat alongside Lewie, and prepared to cut the engines a fraction before touch down, a small task accomplished with great satisfaction. Whistling along the runway, the eternal roar of the engines quenched, we opened the sliding windows to feel fresh damp air beating on our faces. It was great to be alive.

With a final roar of the outer engines Lewie spun the aircraft on the pan to face the perimeter track.

Collecting all our gear, we scrambled out to drop to welcome ground, the gunners with difficulty, having been cooped up so long.

Our ground crew waited expectantly, and with a great babble of voices we attempted to describe to them the details of the night's work. Then followed the ritual handing out of sweets. We rarely got down to eating them. Having unloaded our gear at the various sections, it was time for debriefing.

Upon entering the room, we went straight for the coffee table where a delightful W.A.A.F. asked "with rum?" (the best W.A.A.F.s were always to be found in the most important places).

Drinking our reinforced coffee we waited for the crew in front to vacate the debriefing table. We were already on a 'high', and with the effect of the rum on an empty stomach we became quite garrulous as we all sat down to face the 'top brass' opposite.

We were yet able to give a blow by blow account of our 'trip' and after asking several pertinent questions the Intelligence Officer said, "Thank you gentlemen," and we left the table. We had come up in the world. We were operational.

We hung around a bit, waiting for the huge blackboard to be made up on the return of the other crews who were grateful to have made it. All had returned safely.

We then all went for a quick flying supper, which turned out to be quite a lengthy affair as crews intermixed and starting 'shooting lines' with a new lease of life.

It was daylight as we turned in.

Chapter 2

There was an air of relief next morning as the weather had 'clamped' and all was surrounded in thick Yorkshire fog. 'Ops' were off and we were free to wander about at will. That was the great thing about being on 'ops'. No drill, no bull, and no reporting in or out, so long as we were in a fit state to fly the following night, if required. We enjoyed a leisurely late lunch in the mess. A cheerful affair, as we heard on the radio that it had been a good raid with acceptable losses, 26 aircraft being lost, from one of the largest armadas ever despatched.

In the intelligence room we studied the various bombing pictures laid out under the letter of each aircraft, but they were just impressions of light and dark interspersed with flash trails. They required 'reading' and the intelligence officer was able to point out that we had been in the right place at the right time, as the sky markers showed.

It had been worthwhile. It was a cause for celebration and as we strolled down to dispersal to inspect A-Able we talked of plans for the evening. The ground crew, who appeared to work round the clock, were pleased to down tools and chat about A-Able sheltering under the edge of the wood. Together we discussed the condition of the aircraft; was she all right, any visible damage, hoping at least to find a small hole somewhere.

"No she's good as new," answered Chiefy. "We've been right through her, but we have changed the port aileron which was due for replacement, so you'll be off for a test flight tomorrow if it clears."

I asked if it were possible to have the Lewis gun removed from the nose of the aircraft as it was so draughty and he promised to have a word with the Engineering Officer when he came round to check the numbers of serviceable aircraft.

We had a shave, put on our best blue and were away. We had been to Doncaster on several occasions and sampled most of the pubs, so we went to York and wandered the old narrow streets with a heightened sense of appreciation and interest.

We walked the silent aisles of the Minster and marvelled at the structure of the roof, the enormous pillars and soaring arches, and the skill of the craftsmen of ages past. We had a different sort of craft, but felt committed to defend the beauty of our surroundings. We rounded off the evening in the Crown, surrounded by the paraphernalia of aerial war, photographs and signed caricatures of crews from the many squadrons surrounding the city. It was a fitting shrine to those who had perhaps already gone, and to those like ourselves who were keeping up the tradition.

Next morning dawned bright and clear, with a little light cloud and after reporting to our various sections to keep up with the latest 'gen', found we were down for the air test on A-Able.

With the usual obligatory ground inspections completed we took off in happy mood. We always enjoyed these short test flights, the 'halibag' light and unencumbered, lifting clear from the runway in half the usual distance to rise quickly to our prescribed height.

All the usual evasive manoeuvres were carried out, probably more rapidly than usual due to the fact that we were travelling light, when we found ourselves upside down in the half-roll position.

We had just gone into the corkscrew when the aircraft failed to respond to the controls and we finished up on our back and diving out of the half-roll in the opposite direction.

We hung on grimly, the aircraft shuddering under the unaccustomed load. At probably over 300m.p.h. we entered the cloud below.

We were now lost, the instruments haywire and the artificial horizon out of sight. With superhuman effort Lewie hauled back the wheel for what seemed ages, and the 'G' force was immense, when suddenly we broke from the cloud straight into the sun.

There was a stunned silence, we gathered ourselves together and Lewie levelled off as we checked for injury.

"What happened Skipper?" from one of the coherent members of the crew.

"I've no idea," he replied. "She just refused to come back on the other tack. My arms are about four feet long! I think we'd better go home."

We were to appreciate the great strength of the Halifax, as aerobatics were not written into the design of a heavy bomber.

We returned to base so that 'Chiefy' could go over the whole 'kite' again, to discover to our relief that the incident was entirely due to a malfunction of an aileron 'stop'. He assured us that he had never known it to happen before and it would certainly never happen again.

Satisfied with this promise from the expert, I reminded him again about the removal of the Lewis gun from the nose.

Two days later we were briefed for Frankfurt.

Nobby recorded airborne 20.15 hours and almost at once we were in wispy cloud, which thickened as we laboriously gained height towards the Belgian coast. Our course was directed towards the Ruhr Valley, where it was hoped the enemy would concentrate his fighters, while we changed direction yet again.

On this trip I was saddled with the additional task of throwing out 'window' at regular intervals. These strips of silver paper were to be dropped at regular intervals to confuse and blur the enemy radar, and the front of the aircraft was packed high with boxes. There was a chute now fitted near the escape hatch through which this stuff was to be pushed. Anything that confused the enemy was worth trying, but we were not convinced its effectiveness was ever proved, and there was a theory that our presence could be more immediately apparent.

Over to port, someone had strayed into the Cologne defences and was paying heavily for not changing course earlier. A mass of waving searchlights and winking flak were concentrated on one point. It was not safe to fly alone.

We had changed course for Frankfurt when the weather cleared, and I could easily pick out the curves of the Rhine, and immediately below, the extended row of twinkling lights denoting an enemy fighter aerodrome. Orange coloured balls of tracer rose slowly, suddenly accelerating like Roman candles to fill the sky with exploding sparklers.

There was a lot of muck ahead, but the target area was a disappointment, no coloured lights and no welcoming markers to be seen. A cloud of waving searchlights followed the wave of bombers passing over, and below a glowing mass, heaving with the slow red glow of exploding block-busters.

I called, "How are we for time Nobby?"

"Probably a few minutes late," he replied, "though it shouldn't make much difference at this stage of the proceedings." Then Lewie cut in, remarking that as we were in the last wave, the ground markers had most likely been obliterated by earlier bombing, and we should go for the central area. We were then bathed in sudden light. Two searchlights had coned us and almost immediately, two more following their radar, homed in on us.

My night vision gone, I was temporarily blinded, amazed at the power of the light and the breadth of the beam; even at our height I could read the small print on the bomb-sight and stark shadows flew across the interior of the aircraft.

Lewie put her on one wing tip and we dropped violently into the welcome darkness below, uncaring of any other aircraft in the vicinity. It was a case of every man for himself, in an effort to avoid the inevitable flak at the apex point.

On pulling out of the dive, we had lost 5000 feet and pushed for time, I rapidly reset the bomb-sight accordingly. Other bombers had not been so lucky. The brightest glow in the sky, we now knew, was the signal for another stricken aircraft.

We proceeded in a weaving motion to lessen the chances of being picked up again, dropped our bombs and sped clear.

I remembered what we had been told at briefing, never on any account to let yourself think a searchlight would lose you. Immediate evasive action was the only answer, as within seconds, other beams would be vectored on, together with heavy flak all under the one radar control.

The enemy had got it down to a fine art. They had had plenty of practice and were now using a pale blue master beam which controlled a large area of defences.

The return flight was cold, but uneventful and crossing the English coast I called up Nobby to give him a fix, "Essex coast, Bradwell Bay in sight Nobby, bright and clear." Now with I.F.F. on and with the last alteration to course, we were on the straight run for home. Bradwell Bay was one of several 'lame duck' aerodromes scattered along the coast line, brightly lit by flares, to be used only in dire emergency.

On calling up base on R.T., we were warned to douse navigation lights and circle as enemy fighters were in the vicinity. These intruders had been known to shoot down returning bombers actually over the aerodrome and about to touch down.

Finally we received the all clear, by which time half the squadron was on the circuit and anxious to land.

Not all Snaith aircraft had yet returned, but we hoped these might have landed away, for various reasons.

The Tannoy had woken us at midday, "Report to Briefing 1600 hours, 1600 hours." We scrambled out of bed confused and surprised as rain was lashing the windows, driven by the winter wind.

It was to be Leipzig, and although the weather was foul, we were assured by the Met officer that it would be clear over the target, and improve generally as the cold front passed through. The discussion which followed highlighted our misgivings.

"Bomber Harris has decided," remarked Nobby, "as long as conditions are clear over target, we go!"

"To hell with what it's like when we get back," added Ted, and we all felt that there was some truth in this.

After a hurried flying supper we gathered all our gear together and scrambled into the waiting wagons.

It was almost dark and having witnessed the usual blessing of the engines, we took off in heavy rain and within seconds we were enveloped in cloud. Undercarriage retracted, we bore upwards at 200 feet per minute, now flying entirely on instruments, buffeted from time to time by other bombers flying ahead.

We had been warned to keep clear of the Frisian Islands which, according to the latest intelligence, now bristled with guns and searchlights. Our course would take us to the north and then south-east leaving Bremen on our port beam.

It was a long lonely flight over the North sea and I remembered our recent dinghy drill at the Goole baths where we were told to jump off the top diving board in full flying gear and 'Mae West', hold our noses and drop into the water, before attempting to climb into a large inflated dinghy. It was so horrible and so difficult owing to the weight of our water-logged flying gear that we put the whole idea to the back of our minds.

The sparkle of intermittent gun fire below reminded me that we were now crossing the German coast. Nobby called, "New course coming up Skipper. Alter course 125 degrees."

"OK navigator, 125 degrees it is, turning now."

As we pressed on, the cloud began to break up and in the wan light of the moon I was able to pick out the great expanse of water reaching down to Emden, and with my maps before me, trace the intricate shape of the huge estuary. I scrambled along to Nobby's curtained off 'office', shaded my eyes against the unaccustomed brightness and helpfully pointed out our position. He gave me a sly smile and with a thumbs up, pointed to his chart. He was dead on and we had already flown over 300 miles.

It was now a beautiful clear night, the stars shone frostily and the Milky Way was a translucent cloud above.

With the comforting roar of the engines in my ears I began to look ahead to Christmas. It was unlikely that the base would be shut down, but our crew was due for leave and it could coincide. Perhaps my brother Dick who was now in Ferry Command, flying new American bombers from Canada to Prestwick in Scotland, would be able to fiddle a flight to bring him home on leave.

My reverie was abruptly shattered as A-Able slid violently sideways to escape the exploding orange mass above. Lewie had reacted instinctively to skew us out of the path of the debris of the falling conflagration as it passed our wing tip, trailing burning fuel all the way to the ground, far below. Was it always to be someone else catching it? Had we a charmed life? Every crew believed they would make it, as all around others fell, and it was this belief that kept us going.

"Keep a sharp look out chaps!" Lewie warned the gunners. "There are obviously fighters in the stream, because there's no flak." We needed no encouragement, shocked by the suddenness of death on such a perfect night.

We were now flying almost directly for Berlin, but would alter course for Leipzig, as Mosquito fighter bombers carried on to Berlin to create a diversion. This, it was hoped, would draw the fighters away from the main force.

From time to time the Skipper would call up the gunners to ensure that they were wide awake, while skilfully weaving the bomber from side to side to discourage attack, and increase viewing area.

"How long to target, Nobby?" enquired Lewie over the intercom.

"Zero hour 20 minutes, Skipper, you should be able to see something by now."

To the west, huge candelabra flares, suspended on parachutes, descended lazily to the earth, dropped probably by Heinkels 111s flying above the Mosquitos already attacking Berlin. Ahead was the unearthly pulsating glow of the target area.

We were in the first wave, but the pathfinders were collecting the first of the flak, as they did their timed runs using H2S. H2S could compare to an inverted type of airborne television.

The main mechanism was housed in a large cupola under the aircraft, sending out rapid pulses which in turn were collected back in a huge bowl and transferred to a screen in the navigation compartment.

Working properly, the screen gave an accurate picture of the ground below, greatly enhanced where there were strong features such as hills, rivers, and large towns. We were now in the thick of it, bombers skimming across, above, and below, dog-legging to lose time, thinking they were early as no target indicators were yet visible. Our eyes were everywhere, Rebel, the mid-upper gunner, giving a running commentary as Halifaxes and Lancasters repeatedly changed position in close proximity on the run in.

The flak was intense, the sky a mass of waving searchlights illuminating the smoke of the shell bursts.

And suddenly to starboard, the welcome sight of the ground markers, bright green explosions in the darkness below. We should be one of the first to bomb.

Lewie turned onto the greens, as I called, "Bomb doors open," and I listened for the clang beneath me as the doors swung back.

I had already checked and re-checked the bomb-sight settings and the release gear and was confident of a copy book result, when my night vision was shattered. Directly below, a Halifax had taken the worst kind of hit, in the wing tanks. It was burning with increasing ferocity as the intense heat dissolved the wing which blew off as the aircraft turned over.

Temporarily blinded by the glaring flash, I was only just able to gather myself together to complete the bombing run.

I was reminded of our briefing. There would be upwards of 200 bombers passing over the target indicators in the space of 12 minutes, and all over an aiming point of perhaps 100 yards across. We bombed with difficulty, jostled out of position, and buffeted beyond endurance as with "Bombs gone, Bomb doors shut", we increased 'revs' and turned away from Leipzig.

It seemed a long cold journey home, fortunately unmolested. I was glad that 'Chiefy' had removed the useless pea-shooter from the nose of the aircraft and filled the hole thus cutting down the draught.

We passed north of Frankfurt, where heavy flak and searchlight activity denoted the unfortunates who had been carried south by a change in the wind direction. Nobby had foreseen this possibility when we had arrived too early on target, and had adjusted our homeward course by nothing more than a well judged guess.

Landing early, Lewie shut down the engines and we relaxed gladly, suddenly aware of the silence of the empty aerodrome, the fresh morning air exhilarating. It was still dark, and while waiting for the transport to collect us for debriefing, we handed out the uneaten sweets to the ground crew and chatted about the possibility of arranging a joint night out, all fourteen of us, to be held in the local pub.

We had been in the air for nearly eight hours, but after debriefing and the usual tot of rum in the coffee, we felt rejuvenated, exchanging experiences with the other crews, as we waited for the operations board to be made up. Two slots remained uncompleted, silent eloquence to those given no 'time of return'.

We listened avidly next day to the reports on the wireless in the mess. It had been a highly successful raid. The Junkers factory on the outskirts of the city had been largely destroyed. In the intelligence room later, we were able to examine our own aerial photographs and those of the P.R.U. Mosquitoes who had been over the target at first light to record the destruction. A total of twenty four bombers had not returned, of which fifteen were Halifaxes.

There were now several new faces in the mess, replacement crews to bring the squadron back to strength and I was delighted to find among them my old friend Rod Shaeffler. Rod and I had been among the group re-mustered from the pilots' course in Georgia in a temperature of 100°F to Ontario, temperature zero all in the space of four days, to commence retraining as bomb-aimers.

Owing to the vicissitudes of the service and the intermediate training, he had at last finished up at Snaith and was yet to do his first 'op'.

"What's it really like?" he asked. "Is it as bad as they say, or is it all bullshit?" I hesitated to tell him what it was really like, because every man has a different impression, and anyway I did not want to dampen this happy occasion.

It was time for the Sergeants' mess Christmas dance, and as flying was off due to Yorkshire fogs, everybody was engaged in smartening the place up for the affair.

Though few of us were accomplished dancers, we had no doubt that with a few 'jars' inside us we would be able to get round with the best of them.

We were determined to have a go, particularly when the two W.A.A.F. sergeants from the map-room, Eleanor and Jean, appeared unescorted. Having hung about the map-room on numerous occasions we felt we knew them quite well, and were soon all doing our best to keep up with the band, drawn from all quarters of the squadron, giving their own impression of the Glen Miller sound. Everything became very noisy, with the bar in full swing and the musicians plied with drinks in lieu of other reward.

Now that the weather had clamped down for two or three days, we felt totally relaxed, and Nobby and I walked the W.A.A.Fs home to their billets some half mile away from the main building.

We learnt that they were rarely free at the same time, as one or the other were on duty at various times. Having noted the telephone number of the 'Waafery', Nobby and I returned elated to our quarters, rather enjoying this new phase in our lives.

I had somehow already become drawn to Eleanor, and although we were all deeply enmeshed in the close comradeship of our crews, there was another side to life and perhaps we should make the most of it while we could.

Life on the squadron went on, new crews arriving constantly, so that one hardly had time to get to know them before their faces had disappeared from the mess.

The warm front passed through, and as there was no moon, and the nights clear and frosty, the squadron was put on 'stand-by'. We hated the uncertainty of waiting about, unable to leave the base, unable even to drink to pass the time.

Checking in at our various sections it soon became evident that something was cooking, and then Lewie came out of the 'A' flight office and said that 'ops' were on.

Shortly afterwards, the Tannoy announced briefing at 1500 hours and we began the usual round of preparations.

At briefing, Frankfurt was again to receive our attentions and that as, according to the 'met' report, it was to be cloudless over the target, 'Parramatta' would be used. This was the code name of the system whereby the pathfinders dropped coloured markers which exploded on impact, giving theoretically the exact aiming point for the main force coming along behind. When everything worked perfectly, their H2S and other aids in tune, this was a remarkably accurate method.

We had already started engines and begun the warm up procedure when a red 'Very' light rose slowly from the control hut at the end of the runway. It was 'off'!

Lewie shut down, and we waited in the ensuing silence, strangely disappointed. Now that the moment had come we felt cheated.

Soon appeared a little van calling at each bomber in turn with the latest 'gen'. We were to wait for further orders. Visual signals from the control hut were the only method of communication at the take-off stage, as any wireless signals could be intercepted by the enemy, even from the ground. There appeared to be no urgency and we scrambled out of the aircraft to yarn with the ground crew in the last glow of the evening sun, now wishing the whole affair was over.

We thought better than to make final arrangements for our joint party, as that might be tempting fate, and so the conversation drifted around every day things, the course of the war, and the exciting topic of the preparations for the invasion. As dusk fell we began to think of other things, of home and Christmas leave, when suddenly the darkness was rent by the soaring green flare from the control hut and there was no more doubt.

In sober mood we clambered back into our positions, restarted the engines and taxied out to join the stream of bombers, now with navigation lights on, as they rumbled towards the runway.

At rapid intervals we took off into a frosty sky, engines roaring, 'props' in fine pitch to gain height before crossing the Dutch coast, navigation lights off. We had already turned on our I.F.F. to allay suspicions from our own ground gunners, and in particular the Navy who were renowned for their zeal.

Upon crossing the Dutch coast, Lewie switched on 'Monica', a new radar device set in the tail of our aircraft to help pick up approaching fighters, as the conditions were near perfect for the enemy. Its almost incessant bleeping drove us crazy as it was unable to differentiate friend from foe, and at this early stage the phalanx of aircraft astern were more likely to be friendly. But we could not be sure.

A great strain was therefore put on Johnny in the rear turret to put our minds at rest, whenever he could be visually certain. Later on in the vast wastes of the sky, it was to prove invaluable.

There was no gun-fire, but ominous glows in the clear sky ahead denoted that the enemy fighters were already in the bomber stream, and that the diversion at Mannheim was not yet having the desired effect of drawing off the opposition.

At our turning point, great clusters of fighter flares magically appeared, their smoky trails clearly visible as they drifted down wind. The enemy seemed unusually well informed. 'Monica' now commenced bleeping rapidly, and Lewie put A-Able into a heavy weaving motion, a second before Johnny shouted, "Corkscrew - corkscrew port Skipper!" but no one else saw the fighter, so perhaps Johnny's overstrained eyes imagined the fearsome shadow. Anyway, if in doubt it was better to take action and none blamed him.

The Ruhr Valley (also known as 'Happy Valley' or 'Flak Alley') was now on our port beam, forever filling the sky with muck, and there always seemed to be someone to wake the defences, mostly by accident, rather than design.

We already knew where to make our turn onto the target run, as the enemy was there before us, dropping flares as before. It was uncanny and unnerving. These parachutes flares were glaringly bright, and being visible for over twenty miles enabled the enemy fighters to concentrate on a given point and so mix with the bomber stream.

I was in the nose of the aircraft when straight ahead appeared a sudden glint of reflected light. Approaching rapidly, an enormous greenhouse affair set between two huge engines passed below us at high speed, to disappear rearwards. A-Able rocked and shuddered in its slip-stream.

It was all over in a split second, but my mind was able to register the long ugly perspex cockpit of the Heinkel 111. I inwardly shook; our joint approach speed would have been in the region of 500mph as it passed under us within twenty feet, travelling in the opposite direction. Our closest 'near-miss' to date. Gathering my wits, I called up Johnny in the rear turret, "Did you see what I've just seen, Johnny?"

"Yes I saw it, but too late to do anything about it."

"Nearly knocked me out of me turret!"

There was a good deal of chat following the near-miss, as no one else had witnessed the apparition, and as we settled down Nobby reminded us that it was ten minutes to target. Contrary to what we had been told at briefing, there was now 8/10 cloud over the target area and it was apparent from the mass of airborne coloured lights some miles ahead that pathfinders' were in fact using 'Wanganui'.

This discovery did not affect our method of attack, except that when in doubt we were to go for the brightest sky markers in view, rather than those fading into obscurity in the smoke below.

But there were no new markers. We were now continuously weaving, Rebel in the mid-upper turret keeping a sharp look-out for bombers too close above us, and fighters behind. Though there was no moon there was enough glare in the night sky from the searchlight lit cloud below to show us other bombers weaving and jinking their way through.

We were kept alert by the buffeting from our fellows in front, the screeching of 'Monica' and the all too frequent sudden glow of exploding bombers ahead. I called, "Bomb-doors open," ready for the new markers which did not come. Through the gap in the cloud below I could follow the pin pricks of the bomb-bursts and the red glow of the block-busters, as they swelled into orange mushrooms of light.

Nobby called, "What's the hold up?" as shut away in his little 'office' he was totally unaware of our problems up front.

Heavily shaken by accurate flak-bursts I could sense the rising impatience to be gone, all waiting for the magic words.

With a violent lurch, Lewie flung her starboard to line up with the glaring green sky markers suddenly cascading down ahead. "Left, steady," I called, the markers already jumping about in the tram-lines of the bomb-sight and rapidly nearing the point of release. "Left, steady, steady. Bombs going," and then, "Bombs gone - bomb-doors shut," I shouted, suddenly breaking into a sweat after the urgency of the last few seconds and the necessity of getting the bombs away before we overshot.

Temporarily blinded by the close proximity of the shower of vivid green markers, I was glad to shut my eyes before checking that the ring of lights on the control box had all gone out, and that all was well. I had the impression that things had not gone according to plan;

the attack was widely spread, and as we left the target there was another large glowing area to the South.

Strings of blue tracer continued to crisscross the sky and Lewie warned the gunners to keep awake on the long trip home, as the night fighters were still with us.

The Mannheim diversion to draw off the enemy had obviously not had the desired effect and we were harried all the way up the first leg out of the target area.

Crossing the North Sea, we enjoyed our coffee, and scrambled about removing layers of gloves and warming our hands on the hot cups.

Now that we were losing height for home, we were able to remove our oxygen masks and relax, apart from the gunners who had to remain in their turrets.

It was a difficult task, carrying a cup of coffee the whole length of the aircraft, over and under innumerable obstacles to arrive at Johnny in the rear turret. On arrival, Johnny had to line up his turret with the aircraft and open his rear steel doors, his only entry. In emergency he was supposed to open them to the outside air and roll out, having taken the precaution of first raising his four Browning machine guns to the vertical position to allow rotation of the turret. All this, so long as the main hydraulics were still working. We did not envy him his lonely position.

On our return the weather had remained clear over England, and having turned on our navigation lights and I.F.F., a necessary precaution as the army had no compunction about firing on anything airborne, we crossed the coast, just south of Spurn Head.

The welcome sight of the many flashing beacons giving the call-sign letter of their respective bases was an uplifting sight, and homing on Snaith beacon we joined the circuit and landed quickly.

As always, the incessant roar of the engines silenced, we were at once aware of the palpable stillness, and the return to normality.

We laughed and joked with the ground crew as though we had never left them, and arranged the 'do' for the following evening.

At debriefing we complained about the lack of continuity of the marking over the target, and were assured that this was due to the sudden weather change, and that the lesson has been learned.

It was not easy to unwind, but finally we were able to sleep, as we were now well accustomed to sleeping at the wrong times.

Waking late the next day, too late for lunch in the mess, we resorted to the N.A.A.F.I., to find several other crews sampling the delights of that ubiquitous establishment. The tea was dreadful, but the food was good.

The news had gone round that leave was soon to be posted up on the board, and everyone was anxious to get the 'gen'.

The conversation turned naturally to the relative shambles of the night before, and we learnt that some crews had arrived to find no markers at all and had been forced to drop their load in the general direction of the target.

All agreed that it had been a hairy trip and some had returned with cannon shell holes, fortunately in 'safe' parts of the aircraft. There was a rumour that we had lost three crews. In the intelligence room later, we found the rumour to be a fact, and we were anxious to find out if any had landed away, but no news had come in.

The intelligence officer explained the photographic results of the night's work and informed us that the enemy had lit a huge decoy fire five miles south of the city, and this caused some confusion to the main force.

We learnt that from a total of 650 aircraft engaged, 41 were lost, of which 27 were Halifaxes. Following this depressing news, we were delighted to find that our crew were to be free from all doubts and anxieties for a fortnight.

Leave was posted, and a large number of crews were named in the list, including my old friend Rod, who had now completed his third 'op'. This was a time for celebration, and bicycles were begged, borrowed or stolen from far and wide.

There were fourteen of us including the ground crew, as we set off on a motley collection of machines, some bearing the numbers and colour codes of their respective sections, to which finally they would be returned, in all probability of their own volition.

As far as aircrew were concerned bicycles were common property. We had set off early in an untidy gaggle to the village of Snaith in order to commandeer the small private room in the local pub, before others made a claim.

Normally there was not a great selection of food on offer, but the landlord, having had prior warning, contrived a gigantic feast, its origin unknown. As the evening progressed and large quantities of beer appeared and disappeared almost as quickly, other crews arrived and attempted to take over our domain.

The resultant battle only added to the spirit of the evening, and in the end we were forced to bring into action the added weight of the raddled piano.

'Time' was never called, but to ensure a constant supply of the essential fluid, great old-fashioned enamelled jugs were pressed into use and placed under the table to reappear as required.

Speeches were called for, and 'Chiefy', manfully supported by the ground crew, loudly proclaimed that in his twenty years of R.A.F. service, we were the best aircrew he had ever had the honour to serve, that A-Able was the best aircraft on the squadron and that we were to make sure that it remained so, with his help. Exhausted by his efforts, he fell back among his henchmen, cheered to the rafters.

Amid incoherent shouts and backslapping, the party broke up and we were glad to have been able to show our deep appreciation of the ground crew's work.

We were the last to troop out of the pub into total darkness, to discover that our assailants of the evening had 'borrowed' several of our bikes, which had been carefully stacked out of sight in the pub garden. It was a scene of utter chaos and good natured argument. Who was going to 'double-up' on the remaining bicycles, and who was going to do the pedalling? The ground crew insisted that as we flew their 'kite', we should pilot the bicycles and they immediately jumped on the nearest crossbar to prove their point.

It was a hazardous ride home with no lights and frequent interlocking of bikes as we swerved about in careless abandon, overloaded in both senses of the word. On approaching base we had the misfortune of meeting up with another crew returning in a similar fashion and the resultant 'prangs' were formidable. Bikes became inextricably locked in the darkness. Pedals bent and handlebars askew, we staggered home to fall into a happy sleep in the knowledge that we would not be flying again before Christmas.

With this wonderful new-found freedom I was ready to enjoy a long planned trip with Eleanor to visit her home town just south of Huddersfield for the day. We had been out several times together on hastily arranged meetings, but these had been difficult to plan.

Eleanor was tall, dark and intelligent and we were already very close, our attachment heightened by the pressures of the times.

After lunch at her home, we wandered the bleak winter moors above Holmfirth enjoying the views of the town below, and the heather dark hills rising on all sides, their slopes outlined by rambling stone walls disappearing into the hazy distance. It was time to enjoy the present and put the future to one side.

We had not spoken much, content to wander the lonely sheep tracks and be far away from war and all thoughts of war.

On the way back she turned, as if with some well kept secret, and announced, "I've got Christmas leave! It's only a week, but I shall see you soon. I'm going to stay with my aunt in Staines for a few days."

"But that's only a few miles from where I live," I replied.

"That's right," she answered knowingly. The future looked suddenly rosy and we returned in high spirits, to catch the train back to Snaith.

Chapter 3

With our passes, travel warrants and petrol coupons carefully stowed away, we were off on the London train. Nobby, Ted, Rod and I travelled together for the first part of the journey, before separating in London for our various destinations.

Although we were given a fortnight's leave approximately every six weeks, home was still a steadying influence and a return to sanity.

Trying to answer the innumerable questions from family and friends about the job we were doing and life on the squadron was difficult, as one hesitated to 'shoot a line' and yet felt it was only fair that they had an inkling of what it was really like. With my friends, who had left school with me to join other branches of the services it was different. We were able to swap experiences and learn about aspects of the war which were entirely unknown to us. They were in the navy, and related daring exploits of regular visits to the French coast to collect information and bring back bits of enemy radar equipment for our 'back room boys' to assess and provide the tactical antidote. There was a whole lot going on, but none of us as yet knew anything about the invasion.

During the previous year, when the enemy bombing offensive had been at its height, we had received part of a delivery meant for Uxbridge, for years home of the R.A.F.

I was home on leave at the time. We were all sleeping downstairs, listening to the now well known drone of enemy Dorniers overhead, already awake, as the nearby gun battery had quickly opened up.

We clearly heard the whistles of the first two bombs which exploded in the churchyard across the road, then the house shuddered as in an earthquake, glass and tiles rained down and we were sharply aware of the outside air fresh on our faces. There were several more bomb bursts in the distance.

It was the middle of the night and it was a strange experience to walk out of the house through non-existent doors. There was a tinkling of glass everywhere. The windows had all gone together with half the roof.

Next morning was a scene of desolation. There was a strong scent of pine woods in the morning air, and my father, to his added horror, discovered that over half of his carefully tended conifer hedge had entirely disappeared.

On the other side of the garden nearer the house, the first bomb had exploded ten feet up in the head of a large pear tree, thus accounting for the enormous blast. The tree, apart from the stump, was nowhere to be seen, but all around, like elephant foot prints were the holes concealing the remains of the demolished branches.

It was ironic that an old shed also destroyed in the blast, contained samples of scissors and knives made in Solingen, the property of a well loved German friend of the family who regularly visited us before the war. From then on, knives and scissors appeared at regular intervals in all parts of the garden.

It was to be nearly a year before all repairs were completed and even then there was still a forlorn gap in the hedge.

My brother had been unable to arrange the leave he had hoped for, but many letters in his spidery hand told of the long hours of boredom spent over the Atlantic, where his navigational skills were essential.

My great love and probably my most treasured possession was my motorbike, a pre-war B.S.A. 'Blue Star' which I had since I started my flying training at Booker. My father had been against the idea, as I had already suffered a serious motor bike accident a few years previously, nearly losing my leg in the process, but was persuaded by my plea that I wanted to enjoy my life while I still could.

It was a source of great enjoyment, and now that I had the necessary petrol coupons, most garages were happy to supply that little bit extra, particularly to servicemen.

I renewed my long friendship with John, whose family kept a butcher's shop in West Drayton, which we were never to leave without a pound of sausages in our pockets.

John was now flying Spitfires, and though too late for the 'Battle of Britain' was thoroughly enjoying the life in a single engined fighter. There was a good deal of rivalry between us, as to who was doing the most for the war effort, particularly when his mother was able to say that her Johnny now had a commission. I was quick to point out that the fighter boys had all the luck, and most of the 'gongs' too!

We laughed a lot, and remembered the days when we flew our home made model aeroplanes on the local green. How the three of us built a Canadian type canoe and paddled all the way along the river Colne to Heathrow, which was then a small grass flying field busy with light aircraft.

And then Rod telephoned inviting me over to lunch, where I was surprised and delighted to see beer mugs on the table, a sight that had been unusual in my own home, until Dick and I demanded it, now that beer had become part of our staple diet, and even my father began to enjoy it.

Rod, the only son of doting parents, lived near Stanmore, and we were soon discussing the quirk of fate that had brought him to meet up with me again at Snaith. The conversation naturally turned to the topic of flying operations and we talked about the last three trips we had been on together, though of course in different crews and different aircraft. I discerned that Rod had not enlarged upon the subject in any detail, and we all fell to discussing life on the squadron in general.

Somehow, my mother, in spite of the difficult times, had managed to lay on the usual Christmas feast for our large family; three girls, plus one husband in the army, and myself, though of course Dick was not with us. There was a considerable amount of teasing from my sisters, who of course wanted to know what Eleanor was like, and whether they would see her before they returned to Somerset.

Their whole school had been evacuated from Acton at the outbreak of war and they were there for the duration, only to return home for special occasions. I was able to inform them that I expected a phone call from Staines at any time, and that if they were good I might bring Eleanor home.

Eleanor rang a few days later and I sped over to Staines, delighted to find her in 'civvies' for a change. It was a pleasant shock, almost as if we were meeting for the first time, as hitherto we had always been in uniform.

At dusk, the air-raid warning had sounded and we listened to the incessant drone of the Junkers bombers as they flew towards London. It was encouraging to hear the sharp reports from the guns in the nearby fields, the sudden flash from the barrels momentarily revealing their positions along the river. I was glad not to be on the receiving end. Later on, as the 'all clear' had not sounded, Auntie suggested that, rather than ride home without a tin hat, perhaps I would like to stay the night, an invitation I accepted, and rang home to acquaint the folks. As it happened, I spent the night in an armchair downstairs in the sitting room, from which Eleanor had been evicted at an early hour, and I was left to myself!

Next morning, rising stiffly from the armchair from which Eleanor had woken me, I had a sudden inspiration. "After breakfast, why don't you come back with me to meet my family?" I suggested. "It's not far, and I can bring you home later."

"I'd love to," she replied, "but I shall have to speak to Auntie, as I'm not here for very long."

Auntie thought it would be all right as long as Eleanor was back well before dark, and we rode off happily, the fresh wind stinging our faces. It was not far, and having lived in the area for nearly twenty years, the fact that most of the road signs had been removed for the duration of the war did not worry me.

As we arrived home, my younger sisters, who were having a late breakfast, disappeared upstairs to tidy up, as they had never met a W.A.A.F. Sergeant, even in 'civvies'. My parents were delighted to meet the object of their son's affection, and would now be able to stick a small additional snap in the corner of my photo, one of a pair, with Dick's at the other end of the sideboard. I remember having my photograph taken, some weeks earlier in Doncaster, where I had given directions that they were to be sent direct to my home if I did not collect them within a fortnight. Fortunately, I was still around and able to collect them.

The girls seemed impressed with the importance of Eleanor's job in the map room, in charge of maps covering the whole of Germany and beyond, and were keen to know all aspects of female squadron life.

In the early afternoon we strolled down to the river where it seemed aeons before, John, Dick and I had launched our canoe and paddled away down river. I described to Eleanor the day we had set off early in the morning with all our food and cooking gear, humping the canoe over various weirs, manoeuvring with difficulty under tunnel like bridges and sweating our way back against the stream. I remarked that it all seemed so long ago, although I was still only twenty three, and my brother three years younger.

Remembering our promise, and the short visit over all too soon, I delivered Eleanor to her anxious aunt, and departed in a sudden cloud burst, one of the delights of motor-cycling.

Early in the new year, we returned to the squadron to find we had just missed a Berlin trip. One more out of the way, and as luck would have it, one to suffer probably the least losses ever occasioned. It was now 1944, and while we had been on leave the squadron had been pretty quiet, though there were now masses of new information laid out in our various sections which had to be assimilated and remembered.

While we had been away, A-Able had been fitted with, to us, the magical H2S, and everyone was very excited about this new wonder. As we were one of the only two crews on the squadron to be equipped with this machine we took it as a direct reward, rightly or wrongly, of our bombing results and thus our endeavours had been rewarded. Other crews looked up to us in envy and wondered when their turn would come.

Although H2S was a navigational aid, it was also useful for pin-pointing the target, and Nobby and I would now be responsible for working the machine either together or separately as occasion demanded.

Whenever possible, the two of us were to be found in the wireless section 'genning' up on the test set and learning how to operate it in the dark. We should not be able to stop to read the directions in the heat of battle!

Every test flight from now on was an excuse to try out our new addition and we marvelled at its accuracy, being able to double check visibly on the ground. It was to be different on 'ops' where one would have to rely on its theoretical infallibility set against the usual navigational dead reckoning.

Now, fitted under the belly of the aircraft behind the bomb doors, was this huge bulbous dome, moulded in perspex in the shape of half an egg. A-Able was obviously pregnant. Inside the fuselage, it was even more difficult to reach the rear, now that there was a large hole cut in the floor to house the receiving bowl, which was surrounded by masses of electric wiring. As the whole affair was said to operate under enormous voltages, we gave it a wide berth, clinging where possible to the sides of the aircraft.

Nobby's department had been fitted up with the magic box, virtually an all green television screen which was re-lit at regular intervals by the revolving scanner. We did not have long to wait before using it in earnest.

The weather had remained foul since returning from leave but the cold front was said to have passed over into the North Sea, and test flying was the order of the day.

Next morning, unknown to us, the teleprinter messages had been filtering down from Bomber Command Headquarters at High Wycombe to the various groups, and then to the squadrons.

We received the Tannoy announcement in the early afternoon, "All crews report for briefing 1600 hours, all crews report 1600 hours." The buzz went round the station that it was a big one, and shortly afterwards tractors, towing rows of trolleys delivering overload tanks to the dispersed aircraft, confirmed the early rumours.

In the short daylight hours the ground crew were encouraged to tank-up, fuel up, and winch up the bombs, before darkness made the job more difficult and dangerous. They worked in all weathers sometimes in the most appalling conditions, with amazing enthusiasm.

Ours was a waiting game, and to fill in the time to briefing we sat about in the mess, read and reread all the magazines in sight, and wrote letters home, knowing that a lot was going to happen before our next leave.

We ambled down to briefing early, to make sure of our front row seats, secure in the knowledge that we had earned them now that we were one of the leading crews. It was the unwritten law that 'sprog' crews started from the rear and worked their way forwards. The chattering ceased suddenly, as the top brass wended their way up through the centre of the packed nissan hut to announce the target, which we had already guessed.

A subdued murmur ran round the room, as the huge wall map was unveiled, not so much as to the target, which was no surprise, but to the method of getting there. "A hell of a long way over the sea," and, "Might as well go to Moscow!" were some of the exclamations heard on all sides.

The CO waved his hand for silence. "The battle of Berlin is still on," he announced. "Tonight we're going for one of the eastern segments of the city. As you know, we have divided up the whole area into sections rather like a huge cake, and we are returning to this section before they can get their factories working again."

"There will be cloud over the target," he continued, "and sky markers will again be used. Do watch out for the 'creep-back' factor. Bomb only on the newest, brightest, markers, before they are carried away down wind. As to the route, I'll now hand over to the navigation officer for his remarks," and he sat down to an expectant hush.

The reason for the unusual routing now became apparent. We would fly for over a hundred miles almost dead east over the sea before crossing the Denmark peninsular, thus avoiding all flak and theoretically we would be out of the range of enemy fighters for most of that time.

The navigators busily noted down the mass of detail regarding courses, timing and return flight, and there then followed the usual notes on bomb load, type of bombs and fuel load. The weather report was generally good and it was to be clear for the take off and return to base. That at least seemed encouraging.

The CO had a final word, and wished he was coming with us, a remark received with some scepticism, but as he had already completed two tours and was still not much older than ourselves, we were prepared to give him the benefit of the doubt.

It was to be a late take off, further to confuse the enemy, so Nobby and I had plenty of time to gather our maps and plan the route with the new H2S in mind.

Following a leisurely flying supper, we joined the chatter in the locker room to commence the laborious business of donning our several layers of cumbersome flying gear. The main topic of conversation was naturally the long flight over water, particularly as we would be returning by a similar route, and none relished the thought of the possibility of 'ditching'. At last the transports arrived, and we were glad the long period of inactivity was over, as we clambered aboard, laden down with the addition of parachutes and dinghy packs.

A-Able appeared monstrous in the dim glow of the ground crew's torches and we took up our positions more by touch than anything else.

'Chiefy' assured us that everything was in order, his voice drowned by the sudden roar from across the air-field of the bombers starting up.

We watched as our own engines flared into life, spouting orange gouts of unburnt petrol, before settling down, each in turn, to a regular tick over. Engine checks over, and with a wave of 'Chiefy's' torch, we taxied out to join the throng lining up for the runway.

The airfield was alive with little red and green navigation lights as aircraft moved and turned onto the runway, ready for take off.

On the runway, while waiting for the release of brakes and surge of power, one trusted that the four great engines would maintain their power and lift us clear of the ground. Any loss of 'revs' at this crucial stage was invariably fatal.

Nobby noted airborne at 2300 hours, as we struggled for height with engines roaring in fine pitch. It was as we were taking up our crew positions that the calamity occurred. Lewie's parachute became snagged by someone's harness, the rip cord pulled and the parachute billowed into the cockpit. With great difficulty, we gathered it all together and removed it to the rear, it being impossible to attempt the repacking as we had no experience of the skill required. This was something of a set-back, but Lewie immediately lightened the occasion by calling, "Someone will have to share with me; we'll go together, if we have to!" This unfounded bravado set off a murmur of nervous laughter, as all appreciated its impossibility. It would be difficult enough to carry out a normal escape through the narrow confines of the escape hatch. We tried to forget the incident, but for the first part of the trip there was little to occupy our minds as we pressed on down the first long leg over the sea.

Nobby and I had secured a good 'fix' on the Yorkshire coast with H2S, but now there was nothing. The screen was virtually blank, the sea giving off little reflection as the scanners beams were deflected away. We would have to wait for the coast of Denmark, before taking regular readings.

I signalled to Nobby that I would leave him to it, and returned to my forward position in the nose. It was a clear night, and the stars shone coldly, as there was very little moonlight.

To the north, the convoluted curtains of the Aurora Borealis descended slowly down the sky, the lacy edges outlined in the palest orange changing into blue and green as they faded and returned even more brightly.

It was the first and probably the only time we were to see such a magnificent display and I called up the rest of the crew to witness this strange phenomenon. We had never flown so far north and would shortly be flying over the neck of Denmark before turning south for the target.

Searchlights suddenly appeared ahead, great clusters of beams roving the sky as the first bombers approached the coast. The enemy was clearly determined to protect the Kiel canal. It was an important naval base.

I joined Nobby in his 'office' and together we fiddled with the H2S to get an accurate fix on the islands off the coast, at which point Nobby gave the Skipper a slight alteration of course to take us clear of Kiel.

Seeing the conflagration ahead, others had decided on the same move, and were now passing across our bows, causing considerable buffeting. The night sky was now lit with shell bursts as the earlier bombers proceeded on their way, weaving heavily to avoid the concentration of searchlights.

An urgent 'bleep-bleep' from 'Monica' over the intercom brought us to the alert, but Johnny reported all clear as Lewie commenced the usual weaving motion as a precaution. I returned to my forward position, not enjoying the feeling of being cooped up in the centre of the aircraft unable to see exactly what was going on.

The Met men were right in their forecast, clouds were building up below, their tips visible in the pale moonlight, as we flew into the tail end of the cold front. The incandescent glow of a blazing bomber reflected off the clouds, reminded us that the enemy was already with us. A glare of fighter flares hung suspended in our path as we prepared to turn on to the target run, turning night into day, illuminating the massive build up of the cumulo-nimbus like the peaks of a mountain range, through which we were about to fly.

Occasional lighting split the clouds as we bumped about in the changing air currents. Static (St Elmo's Fire) sped about the metal frames of the perspex nose like small blue sparks, outlining the whole affair. It was unnerving but relatively harmless, and I fell to wondering where it would finally earth itself.

As we made our turn, an unearthly glow above turned into a stricken bomber, probably a Lancaster, which fell past us to fill the cloud below with fire.

There were now ominous orange glows on all sides, made hideous by the reflections on the thunderheads which reared up to engulf us. The enemy, with its radar directed fighters, flew unerringly through the storm unaffected by loss of vision. Surging air currents carried us upwards momentarily, to drop us alarmingly into subsequent troughs so that A-Able shook and rattled as we ploughed through the chasms between the thunderheads. We had not so far experienced the power of this other enemy.

'Monica' so long somnolent, commenced bleeping intermittently, and we braced ourselves for the attack, which did not come. Johnny in the rear turret called up, "Halifax astern, Skipper, I can see the glow from the engines. All OK."

"Thanks, Johnny. Do remember to keep a sharp lookout below," replied Lewie.

Ahead, massed searchlights flickered through the clouds as we approached the first defences. "Five minutes to target, Skipper," called Nobby. "We're only a few minutes late."

"OK Nobby, better late than too early," he replied.

The markers were already vaguely visible ahead, the clouds glowing in suffused ever changing colours. Johnny's yell coincided with the shriek from 'Monica'. "Corkscrew port, corkscrew port!" and Lewie flung the kite to port in the first surging movement of the corkscrew. We hung on, anticipating the upward crushing pressure in the other direction as the plane described a wide arc through the encircling clouds. "We've lost him," yelled Johnny, and Rebel in the mid upper turret confirmed that the fighter had broken away to starboard travelling too fast.

In the cloud laden confusion ahead, it was difficult to judge as yet where the target was, and not to be taken by surprise I called Lewie, "bomb doors open," and he answered quietly,

"Bomb doors open," almost as if I was asking him to pass the sugar. He was as unshaken as ever, and a great calming influence on all of us.

A sudden rosy hue lit the clouds as two bombers went down together, both on fire, probably the result of a collision after one had been shot up. Beads of incendiary cannon fire continued to hose across the sky in between the towering clouds, and from time to time other aircraft were visible as they appeared and disappeared just as quickly.

I switched on the bombing gear and again rechecked the bombing panel, as it was essential that bombs should leave the aircraft in a certain order so as not to upset the flying trim. It seemed that we had been buffeted by the weather for hours and now we had the added discomfort of being caught in the slipstream of other aircraft all proceeding to that as yet unknown release point in the sky.

Through an eerie tunnel of cloud reflected light, tinged green by sky-markers, and rosy red from the fires below, we flew, searching for something to aim at. And then, after a few seconds we broke free from the drifting clouds into a valley of glowing turmoil. Searchlights lit the valley floor in reflected light illuminating the cloud masses travelling downwind with us, to reveal a welcome shower of green markers. There would not be another opportunity. "Right - Right," I found myself shouting. "Steady," as the scintillating mass drifted on to the end of the bomb-sight tramlines, jumping erratically from side to side as A-Able staggered and bumped along in the rough conditions.

"Steady. Steady," I continued, knowing that the aircraft would continue on a mean course despite the deflections, and was rewarded when the green glow appeared against the cross wire, and I was able to press the tit.

Watching the points of light quickly disappearing on the bombing panel, I called Lewie, "Bombs gone - bomb doors shut," and he repeated the message as A-Able surged upwards, suddenly relieved of her load. Having checked that all the bombs had actually left the racks, I relaxed a little, though we were not yet clear of the huge target area. There would be another five minutes flying time before we could slip into the waiting darkness, and head for home. "Halifax crossing from port side Skipper," yelled Rebel from the mid-upper turret, as the huge shape slid across the cockpit, intent to take a short cut home.

This was against all briefing orders. The drill was to continue through the target area before changing course south of the city, all at a given time, thus reducing the danger of collision. This was particularly critical over the target area with a large concentration of bombers intent on carrying out the ultimate aim of the operation.

"Corkscrew starboard Skipper, starboard!" yelled Rebel suddenly from the mid-upper turret, and Lewie turned into the fighter just below, shortening the distance and causing him to overshoot to port. This was the essence of the manoeuvre to give the fighter less time to aim, and less chance to carry on the attack.

Johnny in the rear turret had been unable to see the fighter, which had also been outside the pick-up beam of 'Monica'. Rebel had been lucky - we were all lucky.

The enemy were aware of this blind spot and their pilots knew they had only to lift the nose of the fighter to fill our fuel-filled wings with cannon-shells and though we were equipped with self-sealing tanks, they were no match for cannon shells.

There was no case for hanging about. Lewie put the nose down and increased revs and we sped away through the multi-coloured clouds. Unknowingly, we had improved our chances of getting away clear of the perimeter defences. The heavy anti-aircraft shells had been set to explode all at a predetermined height and we flew through unscathed below the barrage overhead.

Odd searchlights continued to pierce the cloud base, shafting up between the storm clouds. It was still very bumpy, and I recalled the pleasant, peaceful bombing practices we had carried out in earlier days, over Lake Ontario in Canada while training. We were then flying Bolingbrokes, the long-nosed version of the Bristol Blenheim, specially adapted for bombing. It had been very cold, snow lay three feet deep, even on the runway, which was marked by a long row of cut off fir tree tops stuck in the ground.

Although discipline had been strict, life was fun and in near perfect conditions one could attain a very accurate result from the four points of the compass.

Our target had been a floating pontoon in a corner of the lake, painted red. Unfortunately, the roof of a little wooden church a bare half-mile away on the shore line was also red, and several ten pound practice bombs found their mark in the church yard. No damage was done, but the authorities took a dim view and stern measures were taken.

On another occasion, while doing practice feints on one of the many little ships crossing the lake, one bomb-aimer had pressed the 'tit' unwittingly with his control panel in the 'on' position. The string of bombs fell astern of the little ship, but there was hell to pay.

It had been so cold that winter, that any hollow in the camp filled with water one day, became a skating rink by the next morning.

Brought back to reality by a sudden call from Nobby, "How about this then?" I was glad to climb out of the nose of the plane and join him in the comparative warmth of his little 'office'. Together we fiddled with the H2S, taking a fix every twelve minutes, which Nobby transferred to his navigation chart as a double check to ascertain our true position. Anything to help pass the time on the long homeward haul was welcomed. Apart from occasional 'bleeps' from 'Monica' the return trip was without incident, until we approached the Frisian Islands where the coastal defences opened up in strength. Nobby had been able to route us to the north where we had a grand-stand view of the proceedings. Now that the weather had cleared, the bright sparkles of bursting shells were visible for miles, and the sharp pencils of searchlights lit the base of the high cirrus cloud.

As we began the long descent over the North Sea, the incessant roar of the throttled back engines now muted, it was with a sense of relief that we watched the dawn sky lighten to welcome us to another day.

It was coffee time, and while we enjoyed the steaming brew we joked and laughed about the incident of the 'lost' parachute, feeling it was fairly safe to mention the almost taboo subject, now that we were in sight of Spurn Head.

Speeding up the Humber, we were welcomed by the pretty sight of the Hull barrage balloons. While down below, all was as yet in hazy darkness, the balloons above were bathed in the morning sunlight, like rows of little rosy pigs wallowing in the sharp north wind. Lewie altered course to the south, as they appeared to be flying at our height, and we passed over Goole and along the river to Snaith, easy to find in the gathering daylight.

Coming straight in to land, we waited eagerly for the thump of the tyres on the runway, the squeal of brakes, and the deep silence as the engines were at last cut. The ground crew were glad to see us. We were one of the last to land and our sister aircraft, for which they were also responsible, had not returned.

After the rum-laden coffee at de-briefing followed by the flying supper, or rather breakfast, we fell into bed.

Early in the afternoon of the same day word went round that 'ops' were on again. No one believed it. While waiting for definite news, we passed the time in the intelligence room, trying to decipher the bombing photos, which, in view of the weather over the target, proved virtually useless. Perhaps there would be a P.R.U. report once the weather cleared. Our immediate concern was the state of our squadron, which had lost two more aircraft. R.A.F. Pocklington, in the same group as ourselves, had lost five of its fifteen Halifaxes on the same trip. The total losses for this night were thirty five bombers, of which twenty two were Halifaxes.

With this depressing news filling our thoughts, the idea of going again so soon seemed to be tempting fate. And then the Tannoy blared, "All crews report for briefing 1500 hours."

With the details of the previous trip still fresh in our minds, it was difficult to assimilate the new set of instructions thrust upon us.

An early crew photograph at the start of operations.
Sadly, the author and Rebel (standing behind him) were the only survivors.

The 'Terrorflieger' (as enemy propaganda depicted us)
Fallingbostell, Sept. 3rd 1944

Halifax III Bombing-up.

All drawings completed while a P.O.W. and carried from camp to camp and throughout the escape attempt, finally being brought home to England.

Halifax III Taxiing out for Take-off

Dangerous Moonlight

The 'Chop'

POST OFFICE TELEGRAM

Prefix. **1** Time handed in. Office of Origin and Service Instructions. Words. 57

201 1.50 GO/N OHMS PRIORITY 57

PRIORITY=CC MR E A PARTRIDGE WHITE HOUSE CHURCH RD COWLEY MIDDLESEX = DEEPLY REGRET TO INFORM YOU THAT YOUR SON 1388359 F/SGT PARTRIDGE A B FAILED TO RETURN FROM AN OPERATIONAL FLIGHT THIS MORNING STOP LETTER FOLLOWS STOP PENDING RECEIPT OF WRITTEN NOTIFICATION FROM AIR MINISTRY NO INFORMATION IS TO BE GIVEN TO THE PRESS

513/801/165/P1.

No.51 Squadron,
R.A.F. Station,
Snaith,
Nr. Goole,
Yorkshire.

28th. April 1944.

Dear *Mrs Partridge*,

    It is with profound regret that I have to confirm the news already conveyed to you that your Son, Flight Sergeant Partridge, failed to return from an operational sortie.

    He was the Air Bomber, of an aircraft captained by Flight Lieutenant Rothwell, that took off last night to attack a target at Montzen. I regret to say that after take-off, nothing further was heard from the aircraft.

    During the time he had been with the Squadron, he had shown great keeness, zeal and determination and his loss has been a sad blow to us all. Nothing is known of the aircraft, but it is the belief of many of us here, that they would be flying sufficiently high to enable them to make use of their parachutes in time of emergency.

    Meanwhile, his personal belongings have been collected by the Station Effects Officer and in accordance with regulations, will be despatched to you by way of the R.A.F. Central Depository, Colnebrook.

    I should like to explain that the request in the telegram notifying you of the casualty of your Son, was included with the object of avoiding his chance of escape being prejudiced by undue publicity in case he was still at large. This is not to say that any news of him is available, but it is a precaution adopted in the case of all personnel reported missing.

    In conclusion, may I once again express my deepest sympathy in this trying time and reiterate the ernest hope that good news may sonn be received.

Yours sincerely,

for. (C.W.M. LING)
Wing Commander, Commanding,
No.51 Squadron. R.A.F.

Mr. F.A. Partridge,
White House, Church Road,
COWLEY, MIDDLESEX.

Chapter 4

The target was Magdeburg, a small city south west of Berlin. It was immaterial that heavy bombers had not been there before, as the same German night fighters would no doubt be in evidence. There were to be a hundred fewer bombers operating tonight, a grim pointer to the number of aircraft lost or damaged the previous night, some being written off on landing, though the crews may have escaped.

The weather report was good, though this depended on one's point of view, and cries of "Good for who?" arose from some cheesed-off crew members.

Tired and somewhat fatalistic, we were airborne at 2200 hours into a cloudless and frosty sky. It was very cold. Our route was similar to the previous night except that we broke off south east before reaching Denmark, to cross the enemy coast north of Emden.

Night fighters picked us up on their radar as we crossed the coast, and running battles were already in progress before we were halfway to the target. In the long slow glow of burning bombers streaming blazing fuel, but flying on remorselessly, their gunners still firing at the fighters, the picture was revealed. The enemy had already delivered the coup de grace, but hoping against hope that the fires might be blown out, the bombers pressed on.

We now knew by experience that these petrol fires blazed on with increasing ferocity until the wing involved became incandescent, melted and blew off, giving scant time for escape. We were now weaving constantly as a precaution, though "Monica" had so far remained silent.

Lewie called up the gunners, "Keep searching below and on both sides, all the time, chaps."

"OK Skipper," came the reply, both gunners being on tip-toe and scanning the sky in all directions. A stream of incendiaries crossed our bows, but it was not meant for us. The recipient was already on fire.

Things were hotting up and when 'Monica' bleeped, sudden fear gripped us momentarily but subsided as the bleeping faded.

We felt like sitting ducks and fear came and went just as quickly. One cannot be afraid for six hours on the stretch, and nature takes over, allowing the body to relax, except when in extreme emergency.

Finally, this often resulted in a form of mental exhaustion, from which many crews suffered, though more afraid to express their feelings publicly by the possible disgrace of being grounded L.M.F. (Lack of moral fibre).

Nobby called, "New course coming up Skipper, alter course 095 degrees for target."

"New course 095 degrees," replied Lewie, and we banked slowly to port, keeping a good lookout for other bombers. We were now flying almost straight for Berlin in the vain hope of confusing the enemy.

I had now joined Nobby to assist with the H2S, and after a short while, Nobby pointed out that something was wrong. According to the set, we were covering the ground much faster than we should have been, and if the H2S was right, and we had no reason to doubt it, the winds were now much stronger than forecast. As a result, we could be arriving at the target area several minutes early with dire consequences.

"Skipper," Nobby called, trying to keep his voice under control. "We're going too fast, the winds have changed, and the following wind has increased!"

"OK Nobby," replied Lewie, "I'll throttle back a bit, but I've got to keep the old girl airborne! Let me know how we're doing."

Immediately, we were suddenly illuminated by a cluster of fighter flares hanging above us, their swirling smoke trails drifting down wind. Our nakedness suddenly revealed, the night fighters no longer had to search for us, as a larger number of bombers were now visible to friend and foe alike. We were somewhat consoled by the fact that we could also see the enemy.

At the urgent shout, "Corkscrew port, Skipper, Corkscrew port!" I was halfway back to the nose position, and caught unawares was flung about mercilessly, hanging on for dear life. It was impossible to move, as the forces pressed down and then reversed as A-Able swung into the shuddering motion of the corkscrew, and I was determined not to get caught in that position again.

The fighter left us for other prey, but we continued weaving before returning to an even keel. To starboard, Hanover opened up. Searchlights and heavy flak denoted the straying of part of the main force, owing to the wind changes, of which they were unaware. Bombers were caught in the ever searching beams, showing clearly as pinpricks of reflected light, surrounded by the sparkle of bursting shells. We were glad to be out of it, thanks largely to H2S.

But our own course was now lit with a succession of great candelabra flares, turning night into a day even more horrendous. It was an unnerving sight and we began to wonder whether it was all worth it. To come all this way and yet be unable to reach the target seemed pretty pointless.

In the distance, expanding orange glows marked the end of stricken bombers, and close at hand, flaring conflagrations fell away, blazing all the way to the ground, no parachutes visible. A P.F.F. aircraft was among the victims, its position sharply marked by a succession of green and red explosions as its markers surrendered to the intense heat.

For the first time, the enemy were firing strange "Scarecrows" into the night sky, fearsome at first glance but relatively harmless as we were later to discover. These consisted of shells which burst at a prescribed height, sending out a series of other explosions to cover a wide area, rather like a huge firework. The story was, that these secondary explosions were connected by wires in order to bring down bombers crossing their path, a rather illogical but not impossible flight of fancy. They were just trying to scare us, but we were beyond scaring. We had become hardened and fatalistic, intent only to do the job we had been given and to get home in one piece.

Nobby called, "Five minutes to target Skipper, we seem to be back on time," and Lewie acknowledged.

Part of the main force was already bombing. Propelled by the high winds and early, they had relied on their H2S, those that had them, and were not prepared to wait for zero hour and the P.F.F. markers.

With feelings of self preservation uppermost they were swarming through, while the P.F.F. attempted to put their stamp on the proceedings by dropping huge numbers of green and red markers which shimmered and sparkled over the whole target area. It was one of the prettiest sights I had ever seen, although deadly in intent. Splashes of incendiary bombs criss-crossed the glowing scene, interspersed by the pinpricks of the bursting bombs, and anti-aircraft guns.

Held spellbound, I watched this ever changing multicoloured fair ground, and called up Nobby to come and have a look, forgetting that he had never witnessed a target area. He came, looked and retired rapidly to his darkened 'office'. He was happiest with his instruments and had no wish to see the real world.

Calling "Bomb doors open," and switching on the bombing panel, I began to wonder which set of markers to go for. Having marked out a mass of red straight ahead I was content to allow Lewie to continue weaving until the very last moment.

We were by now convinced that weaving, although using more fuel, was the best method of avoiding fighters, who were impatient to get a kill. I could leave it no longer.

"Steady," - I called and then, "Left," as A-Able steadied on an even keel and I pressed the tit. It had become pure habit to go through this somewhat perilous drill, even though the whole operation had by now become a shambles. "Bomb doors closed," I called, unhappy to see that one bead of light remained brightly visible on the control panel.

A pennant of flame streamed suddenly above us, increasing in intensity, to erupt into an immense ball of cascading fire. Lewie hurtled A-Able to one side and we passed through the smoke trail of the whirling nightmare as it fell away past our port wing.

Death in the air became immediately close at hand with the realisation that the crew had no chance.

Silence reigned. The presence of disaster stared us in the face with fear and overwhelming pity for those whose turn had come.

There was no alternative; as Lewie pushed the throttles open, the four engines responding with a higher note, we raced from the scene of destruction. The close proximity of the recent horror had left us with throats dry, and a general feeling of lassitude. It was only due to Lewie's split second reactions that we were still airborne and on the way home.

I now had to announce the unfortunate fact that we had a 'hang-up'. It was unlikely that the bombing panel was at fault. The fact that one small light still remained shining balefully in the darkness, pointed to there being one large bomb left hanging on its hook in the bomb-bay. Disconnecting my oxygen supply, I scrambled rearwards to a position above the bomb-bay, to check visually. In the flickering light of a small torch the 1000 pounder was revealed. The long black streamlined shape, half a ton of high explosive, hung firmly beneath me. I actually had to touch it to be quite certain.

Returning to my forward position, and plugging into my oxygen supply, I took a few long gulps before calling up the Skipper.

Feeling slightly responsible, though in fact the release failure was entirely electro-mechanical and no doubt due to the ever present 'gremlins', I called up the Skipper.

"I am afraid we've got a 'hang-up' Lewie, one of the rear 1000 pounders is still with us. I've made a double check, there's no doubt about it!"

"OK Tony, I was wondering why she was flying a bit heavy," he replied. "I'll open the bomb-doors and go into a bit of a dive, so that you can fiddle with the manual release as I pull up again. We'll try to shake it off!"

Returning to the top of the bomb-bay, I struggled with the release toggles at each successive dive, but with no effect. "We'll leave it for now, until we're over the channel, it may be frozen up," called Lewie, as he closed the bomb-doors, and regained the lost height.

The return flight was fortunately fairly peaceful owing to the fact that the night fighters had remained largely in the target area, though one could never be sure. It was never safe to relax; attack could come from any quarter.

Some crews, belatedly discovering the wind changes, had over compensated and were running the gauntlet, by over flying part of the Ruhr Valley. Probably the most highly defended area of the whole of Germany. "Happy Valley" was notorious for its rapid and accurate response to intruders. The stragglers, probably few in number, were now at the receiving end of predicted fire, which was more frightening than anything else, not only from the visual effect.

On reaching the channel, and before having our coffee, we discussed the possibility of having another try at releasing the 'hang-up'. After repeated attempts with no avail, Lewie called, "We'll have to land with it and hope it stays on! Nothing else for it."

In answer to repeated mutterings from the rest of the crew, Lewie and I tried to assure them that it should be quite safe, as it was not yet armed.

Theoretically it was safe, as the little propellor on the tail of the bomb only flew off after dropping several thousand feet, thus releasing the firing pin and arming the bomb. To prove my point, I reminded them that several Halifaxes had returned safely with large holes in their wings, where bombs, dropping from above had passed clean through.

Still, it was a lot of explosive, though not 'live' in the true sense of the word.

Lewie called up base, and acquainted them of our position, and we were ordered to join the circuit and await instructions. This caused some alarm, as we could visualise the panic precautions on the ground, the bringing out of the fire tenders, and the 'blood wagon' to the end of the runway.

Finally we were clear to 'pancake' and Lewie made a long low approach to touch down with a whisper, but it was not to be. With a great thud, the bomb fell through the bomb-doors and hit the ground to go skidding across the runway in a shower of sparks. Johnny in the rear turret was bounced up and down like a pea in a pod, as the bomb in its passage hit the fixed tail wheel, even before we were properly stuck to the runway, and Lewie had a job in keeping her straight. The ground crew thought it a great joke, an occasion to remember.

We were only the fifth aircraft to land, and they informed us that the rest of the squadron would probably have to land away as the bomb had not yet been found. It would take until daylight to search the length and breadth of the runway.

At de-briefing we were acquitted of all blame. 'Hang-ups' were rare, but we had carried out the required drill, and no-one believed we would have brought back a 1000 pounder H.E. by choice. We were later to learn that one crew had returned with a 500 pounder and had not lived to tell the tale.

The intelligence officer asked for our comments on the trip. He already knew about the massive wind changes, but we were able to describe in detail the visible shambles over the target, when so many bombers arrived before Zero hour, followed five minutes later by the Pathfinders dropping markers in an apparently haphazard fashion.

We mentioned our first experience of the enemy 'scarecrows', and that in our opinion, losses would be heavy, as the night fighters were in full force right from the enemy coast.

Our flying supper was a quiet affair, the ground crew being correct in their prediction that the majority of the squadron would be landing elsewhere. There were at least two other bases within ten miles, and there would be no further news until late in the morning, when we would, without doubt, be the butt of much cursing and blinding.

By lunch time, they had found our bomb, and the diverted crews had all returned.

The bomb had skidded off the runway and buried itself in a drainage ditch at the side of the runway, which accounted for its disappearing act.

The other crews finally accepted our excuses and the story gave us all something else to talk about, other than the dire results of the trip. Fifty seven aircraft failed to return, while the Halifax loss rate was 15 percent. The chances of completing a tour were now whittled down to one in three.

The greatest shock to me was the loss of my friend Rod, of whom nothing had been heard. He had completed five operations, while we had survived twenty. No one knew the answer, as with all the skill and caution in the world, it finally boiled down to just bad luck if you happened to be in the wrong place at the wrong time.

Since having joined the squadron only six months earlier we had been to Berlin five times. and to many targets in the Rhur Valley, almost without a scratch. Some of us had been recommended for a commission, but that would not now come before completion of our tour of thirty operations.

And now the winter snow descended on Yorkshire, and we were not sorry.

The squadron was virtually stood down, visibility fell to a few hundred yards, and the ghostly forms of the snow mantled aircraft stood silent on their virginal pans.

Life took on a new meaning. There was almost a holiday feeling about the place, as mess 'do's' became more frequent and rowdy sing-songs reflected the general atmosphere. The ground crew joined us in another outing which proved even more fraught than the previous one due to the treacherous road conditions, and we did not return to camp until the early hours, mostly on foot, carrying the bicycles over our shoulders, before dropping into bed in a stupor. It was almost like being on leave, and I telephoned the 'Waafery' and asked for Eleanor, sure she would be there, and we arranged to meet at the gate.

We had only been out once since Christmas leave and apart from fairly regular visits to the map room in the course of duty, I had not seen much of her. So it was with happy expectancy that I stood at the gate in swirling snow, waiting. I waited for what seemed hours, by now a statue in snow, feeling somewhat let down, doubtful, yet certain that some unforeseen error had crept into the proceedings. With some trepidation I marched up to the forbidden portals, went in, and asked for Eleanor.

I was immediately surrounded by amused and smiling faces, anxious to help in my enquiries, much impressed that I was well 'out of bounds', and that the matter must be of some importance. Eleanor then appeared, and with much delight and relief, it turned out that I had been waiting at the wrong gate.

The blizzard had now eased up a little, as we strolled among the silent trees, weighed down under their burden of frosted snow. It seemed impossible that just over the hedge, the huge weapons of war stood waiting to fly, awaiting their orders.

We talked about the last few trips, aware that the next one could be the last, though afraid to put it into words. We played with the idea of spending a night together in Selby, in the comfort so much missing from camp life, but decided that it was not important. We did not need to prove a point, moreover, it was courting fate.

It was then that Eleanor dropped the bomb-shell. "I'm posted to Burn," she murmured.

"Where's Burn, and when are you going?" I exclaimed.

"We've heard nothing definite yet, but the new 578 Squadron has been operational for months," she answered. "And they need us to take over the maproom."

"How far away is Burn?" I asked, having never heard of the place.

"It's just ten miles north as the crow flies," she replied, "I looked it up on the map - not very far."

"Could be worse, I suppose. I could always pinch a bicycle, but it's going to make life even more difficult from now on," I remarked.

With this news colouring an already uncertain future, we arranged to get the bus into Thorne the next evening to find somewhere to eat, and make the most of what little time we might have together Leaving Eleanor at her quarters I returned to the main camp in despondent mood, angry at another turn of fate.

Shortly afterwards the snow turned to slush, and in chill March winds, test flights re-commenced in readiness for another onslaught. It was at about this time that we were invited to join the 'Pathfinders', but in a joint decision declined the honour, not relishing the thought of starting a new 'tour' at this late stage.

We flew again to Essen, Stuttgart and Frankfurt while the weather remained favourable. We almost knew by now, from the weather reports given at briefing, what sort of night it was going to be; mainly fighter, or mainly flak, although there was always a bit of both, in every trip.

It never ceased to amaze us that the enemy night-fighters continued to operate very often in the same flak belt as ourselves, at considerable risk from their own gunners below. But in most cases, particularly over the target, the fighters flew in the gap between the heavy flak above, and the quick firing tracer below.

But experience had taught us that no two operations were alike and that each trip was always going to be a flight into the unknown. Towards the end of the month in the lengthening days, overload fuel tanks were again observed by the eagle-eyed, the long strings of the tractor hauled trailers making their way down to the aircraft lined up under the leafless trees.

The tarmac was once again the scene of great activity, bomb trolleys and petrol bowsers trundled from kite to kite delivering their loads and topping up the additional tanks. It was going to be a 'big one'.

We had carried out the usual half-hourly air test on A-Able during the morning and she was perfect, so we were certain we would be going. Though heavy rain clouds raced across the airfield, we knew in our hearts that the weather would not deter 'Butch-Harris'.

The Tannoy boomed that briefing would be at 1500 hours, but as the weather began to worsen, there was a general feeling that the operation might finally be scrubbed, though this was unlikely as the aircraft now stood ready, bombed up, and fuelled up for a specific operation.

A hush fell on the briefing room as the C.O. and the attendant officers came up the narrow aisle between the crews, squashed together on the hard seats or leaning up against the walls. The average age of the crews was under twenty-five and many of the gunners were still in their teens. Some were well into their tour, while others were about to do their first 'op'. It was a time of mixed emotions.

As the C.O. mounted the rostrum the whisper went round "Not Berlin again". But it was not Berlin. It was to be Nuremberg, on the very limit of our range, and during the shortening night hours.

At the first sight of the huge wall map, there were cries of amazement and consternation. Where was the zigzag course to the target, to which we had become accustomed, the frequent changes of course to confuse the enemy? Before us was an almost straight line to the target. There were only two slight alterations to course, after setting off from the Naze, and the second leg was 250 miles long before turning south on the bombing run for Nuremberg.

There was no explanation, it was just assumed that owing to the shorter night and nearly eight hours flying time, crews might with luck be clear of the enemy coast on the homeward leg by dawn.

There was to be a feint attack on Cologne and the C.O. went on to enlarge upon the reasons for attacking this long range target. We were told that since many of the armament factories and electrical works in Berlin had been blasted during the systematic bombing of that city, the Germans had transferred a great deal of their heavy engineering to distant factories, thought to be out of range of the R.A.F.

On this occasion, both 'Wanganui' and 'Parramatta' target indicators would be used according to prevailing weather conditions over the target.

Eight hundred aircraft would be involved, and these were timed to pass over the target in two waves, and drop their bombs all in less than thirty minutes, thus saturating the area. Zero hour was to be at 01.10 hours, but target marking would commence ten minutes earlier with P.F.F. Mosquitos dropping green markers, followed by P.F.F. Lancasters with yet more target indicators and this would be carried on throughout the operation so that the consequential bombing did not obliterate the aiming point. 'Window' was to be used, dropping it, as before, at one bundle a minute increasing to two bundles a minute on approaching the target, further to confuse the night fighters, or so it was hoped.

The intelligence officer reminded us of the known flak concentrations, and warned of a new system that the enemy were now using when confident of the height and direction of the bomber stream. This was the box barrage, where groups of a dozen heavy A.A. guns were deployed to fire rapidly in one particular area of the sky, forming a curtain of flying steel, maintained by H.E. shells arriving every few seconds. The answer was to ram on full throttle and dive straight through, but our thoughts ran on further, able to foresee the chaos of perhaps a dozen bombers carrying out the same manoeuvre in the same area of sky. It did not instil confidence to note that the proposed route passed almost directly over two enemy fighter directional beacons responsible for beaming the fighters into the bomber stream.

The weather report was for local fog on return, but probably ten tenths cloud over Germany and thick layers of cumulus over the target, with westerly wind speeds of 40-50 m.p.h. The promise of heavy cloud over Germany did little to raise our enthusiasm, as we knew that the met men had little information to draw on, and were frequently proved wrong. There was also a rising moon, during which we were normally stood down.

The nervous tension was almost visible as we went for our flying supper. As always before an 'op', conversation revolved around any subject other than the job in hand, and this was no exception. No one had heard of Nuremberg. It was not on our 'map', and no one had been there before. All we knew was it was a hell of a long way, and we did not like the method of getting there.

Time dragged before take-off, and it would only have taken one crew to start ordering drinks before there would have been a rush for the bar. But no one drank just before an 'op', it was courting fate, and besides, there was the dreaded Elsan to consider. One could only imagine the difficulties in crawling to the rear of a rocking aircraft to relieve oneself in total darkness with all hell let loose.

It was with almost relief that the clock took over and we scrambled into the waiting transport for delivery to our various aircraft, dispersed far and wide over the darkened airfield. We waited anxiously for the symbolic blessing of the engines, without which we would not have flown, such was our state of mind. As the time drew near for take-off and the first aircraft received a 'green' for go from the control hut we knew that we were committed. 'Ops' were either on or off, and we taxied on to the end of the runway to await our turn.

Encouraged by the mighty roar and thrust of the four Bristol radials, we surged into the haze at the end of the runway and were at once enveloped in a heavy rain cloud, climbing on instruments.

On approaching the rendezvous over the North Sea it became apparent that already the wind had increased, and Nobby called up the Skipper with a new course based on 'Gee'. This navigational device relied on ground station beams based in England, which were still reliable at short range, though the enemy were now able to bend the beams over Germany. As we turned onto the first leg the weather became very bumpy as we climbed through the rain filled cumulo nimbus and we were alone.

Crossing the Belgian coast there was further evidence of unbelievable wind changes as Nobby and I fiddled with the H2S and secured a reliable 'fix' showing a drift of 15 degrees and a wind of nearly 70 m.p.h. Crews without the benefit of H2S were now being carried rapidly into Germany and would be flying outside the planned concentration. And the mountainous clouds were dispersing.

Nobby clicked on his intercom and called, "Navigator to Skipper. We've got a tail-wind of 70 m.p.h. and unless we dog-leg we're going to be too early at the first turning point."

"Are you quite sure?" enquired Lewie, and on receiving the affirmative, swung the Halifax in a gentle bank, warning every one to keep a sharp look out. Everyone dreaded dog-legs. A-Able would have to fly 60 degrees port for one minute, then swing across to starboard 120 degrees for one minute, so losing one minute in the process. This meant repeatedly crossing the bomber stream until the required time was lost, and although squadrons were given different flying heights, other aircraft were no doubt carrying out the same manoeuvre, which greatly increased the risk of collision.

Back in the bombing position on look out, it at once became clear that the clouds were breaking up, bright stars began to shine, like diamonds in a jeweller's window. Against this backdrop, bombers above were visible at the point of long vapour trails, clearly marking the progress of the stream. And we had only just crossed the enemy coast with over 300 miles to go in almost daylight conditions. It was going to be a fighter-night and with their superior armament of heavy machine guns and cannon they could afford to stand off out of range of our pea-shooter turrets, and blast away at will.

The expected A.A. fire from the coastal batteries had not come, again pointing to fighter activity, and in the added light of the rising moon we quietly cursed the met-men, though fully aware that it was not their fault.

I had by now begun the boring task of throwing 'window' down the long chute next to the bombing position, in the hope of confounding the enemy fighter radar receptors. Anything that might work was worth trying, though crews generally had little faith in its ability now that the enemy radar system was so advanced.

Nobby called for the change of course on to the long leg to Fulda and Lewie banked slowly to port in response.

It was eerily silent, no flak was visible and yet distant orange glows rose and fell ominously. Lewie called up the gunners, "Keep a look out below, because that's where they'll be." No reply was needed, everyone knew that fighters were already among us.

A row of enemy candelabra flames appeared suddenly above us dropping at regular intervals, indicating the course of the bomber stream. In the ensuing brightness the identification letters of nearby bombers were clearly readable, and the night fighters working in pairs, displayed their own hideous black crosses.

We were now flying down an avenue lit by flares as far as one could see, and Lewie was repeatedly having to alter course violently to avoid other aircraft in the final throws of drastic evasive action. The sky became a whirlwind of heaving bombers in all angles of flight, many beyond the flight tested endurance of the aircraft, yet they remained airborne, for the moment of escape, to continue on their course.

It was every man for himself, and when Johnny shouted, "Corkscrew port, go go!" we endured the crushing forces as A-Able fell away and reared up in the opposite direction, as the Messerschmitt 110 overshot and went in search of other bombers.

It was almost impossible for the gunners to rotate their turrets and return fire in the split seconds required, when their own aircraft was gyrating wildly through the sky and few fighters were actually hit during this evasive action.

It was now borne in upon us what this night was to cost Bomber Command. We had just witnessed the hideous sight of a Halifax disintegrating right in front of our eyes, and the consequent horror of having to fly through the funeral pyre was unnerving beyond measure. On the ground we had left a trail of blazing crosses, the last resting place of dozens of bombers. One of our duties was to keep a log of fallen aircraft, but this was not possible. Too many had fallen and it was of no value.

Caught up among the flares were more of the scarecrow rockets the enemy were now using to demoralise the crews into thinking they were bombers exploding. One only had to look down to get the true picture.

The enemy were using everything to alarm and confuse and on the ground, strange shooting stars were visible, and single searchlights guided the fighters onto the bomber stream. It seemed that the enemy knew our every move, almost in advance and that our chances of a safe return were indeed slim.

It was then that I picked up a foreign aircraft in formation with the bomber stream. It was a Heinkel 111 and as I watched I noted that it did not alter course in any way but flew with us at the same speed and direction. Calling the Skipper I said, "Lewie, there's a Heinkel 111 flying with us just below and ahead. Do you think we ought to have a go at it?"

"No, keep your eye on it," he replied. "They know we're here, and it would be impossible to get underneath and open fire without their knowing. Besides, they've got far superior fire power." Finally the Heinkel 111 drifted away and I resumed my look-out and the dropping of 'window'. We were now half-way to the target and if possible, things were getting worse. In the brilliant light of ever descending flares, reinforced as they began to fade, running battles were going on all around us, and tracers continued to come from all angles, as fighters made their attacks and broke away. 'Monica' bleeped almost continually. We were again attacked and corkscrewed repeatedly before the fighter broke off, showering us with spent bullets which rained down on the fuselage like hail on a tin roof. By good fortune the fighter's cannon may have misfired and we flew on unscathed.

Long pennants of flame continued to mark the progress of the bomber stream as more aircraft fell in glowing balls of fire to finish on the ground as fiery crosses, some exploding in green and red stars denoting a pathfinder aircraft.

It was with some force of will that I stopped myself counting the glowing infernos. After witnessing more than 50, the realisation came to me that with a bomb-bay full of bombs and incendiaries, and wings full of fuel tanks there was bound to be a flaming cross.

With strained eyes forever searching the sky ahead, I watched the heroic efforts of a bomber under attack, the fighter coming in left and again from the right, willing the bomber to extricate itself from the almost inevitable end, by superior fire power.

There was little more we could do. Out of the corner of my eye, I could discern Mac the wireless operator feverishly working at his set, attempting to drown the enemy radar by sending out amplified engine noises on their wave length.

Each individual operation had now become the equivalent of a major tank battle or a single naval engagement.

The final turning point, some miles ahead, was already well lit with fighter flares, when a simultaneous shout from both gunners, "Corkscrew port, Corkscrew port!" clawed at our hearts. As Lewie heaved A-Able over, a series of resounding explosions shook the aircraft and A-Able shuddered from stem to stern under the onslaught. The air became filled with the acrid fumes of cordite and an immense draught sucked every loose item from the front of the aircraft. There was no visible fire, and at the gunners' assurance that the fighter had broken away, probably assured of success, we were able to inspect for damage.

Lewie reported that A-Able appeared to be flying normally, and clinging to every available hand-hold to avoid being swept away by the gale, we moved cautiously aft to discover a ragged door-sized hole in the starboard side of the aircraft opposite the engineers' position. Ted lay slumped in his seat, obviously wounded; to what extent we did not know, but we carried him with difficulty past the yawning hole to the rest position. Inflating one of the small dinghies we laid him down in comparative comfort, while inspecting for serious injuries. He was conscious, and although his wounds appeared extremely messy we could just hope it was nothing fatal. Ted was already connected to an emergency oxygen supply and we took great gulps as and when we could from available sockets.

I called up Lewie and told him how things were and what we had done and he replied, "You'd better clip on Ted's parachute!" a suggestion which brought us back with a jerk to our perilous position. He then called again, "Do you want to turn back, chaps, or go on?" There was a unanimous vote to carry on, no doubt partly based on the knowledge that it would be almost impossible to fly against the stream alone. Anyway the worst was over, or so we told ourselves.

It appeared that a string of cannon shells had ripped the hole in the side of the aircraft and carried on, demolishing the astro hatch in their path, thus showering Ted with fragments both of metal and perspex. Had Ted been standing up at the time he would without doubt have received a shell through the head. He was lucky. We were all lucky in that Lewie had already commenced his manoeuvre when the 20mm cannon shells, instead of finding their mark in the wing-tanks, finished up in the fuselage.

We still were unaware of any damage to undercarriage or controls, but for the moment were content just to be still flying.

Recovering from our efforts we began to realise how cold the outside air was, now that it was storming through the aircraft, and after checking the fuel gauges at regular intervals decided that we still had a chance.

Nobby's call, "Alter course for target 065 degrees Skipper," reminded us that we only had a hundred miles to go, about twenty minutes flying time, before commencing the long run home in what we hoped would be blessed darkness.

We had now been flying for nearly two hours in virtually daylight conditions, harassed all the way, with eyes smarting and mouth dry, impatient to get the job done, and be gone.

I called up Nobby and asked for the latest wind-speed and direction to reset the bomb sight, as the original settings given at briefing were miles out. With a horror born of fascination, and a strange detachment, I watched the mindless slaughter as dozens of Lancasters and Halifaxes tried to fight their way to the target, confident that at least we would never be asked to do this again.

As we approached the target, wisps of cloud began to form strata near the ground and 'wanganui' was already visible, glimmering amid the searchlights, with flak sparkling in between. I called up Lewie on the intercom, "Bomb-doors open," relieved to hear his reply "Bomb-doors open," denoting that the hydraulics at least were still in working order. I did not savour the thought of winding them open by hand. On switching on the bombing panel the usual welcome signs of life appeared, and I was ready for a quick release.

Bombers now appeared from all directions to drop their loads and get out while they could. It was obvious by their angle of attack that the high winds had played havoc with their calculations and they were altering course on sight.

Target areas were always difficult, but this was chaos. Immediately below us was a Halifax on its run-in, and it was almost impossible to change position without risking collision, as other aircraft skimmed over and closed in, unwilling to give way, all aiming for a mass of red indicators some two miles ahead.

There was little time, but Lewie managed to slide A-Able to one side as we bumped and shuddered through a sky now pock marked with shell bursts.

Three more bombers fell flaming into the inferno below as we commenced our run in, one gunner still valiantly returning fire from his stricken aircraft. It was a sobering sight and a lesson to those of us still airborne.

Looking through the bomb-sight, I was astounded at the amount of drift we were experiencing. Relative to the markers below, we were all flying crab-wise due to high winds from the west, and it was with some difficulty that I aligned up our aiming point in the tram lines. Calling, "Right and then Steady, Steady," I pressed the tit, knowing that all ears were waiting for the magic words "Bombs gone", and the freedom to be away from the inferno.

As A-Able leapt upwards, relieved of the load at last, Lewie pushed the nose down and rammed on full throttle as he closed the bomb-doors. We might yet be short of fuel, but we had to get clear, into darkness at last. Once clear of the target area, Lewie throttled back and we again checked the fuel gauges.

With the help of an H2S now working spasmodically, Nobby tried to arrive at an E.T.A. for base allowing for a wind speed of now nearly 80 m.p.h. against which we would have to strain all the way home.

There was still some 800 miles to go and if the wind remained at its present force, about four hours' flying time.

Nobby now called up the Skipper. "Skipper, unless the wind drops, we may not make it! Thought I'd better tell you."

"Ok Navigator, I'd ease back a bit, but we don't want to get caught over the coast in broad daylight! How's Ted bearing up?"

"He's OK. He was able to drink some coffee," was the reply.

The shortage of fuel was partly due to the amount of evasive action we had had to take on the way to Nuremberg, and if the winds had been as forecast by the Met men we would have been happy and confident. Other errors soon crept in to increase our anxieties.

Whereas it was to have been cloudy over the target and clearing on the way home, the reverse was now apparent.

Massive cloud banks, indicating a cold front, were now rearing up ahead, their mountainous peaks towering above us. Despite the threat of icing-up, Lewie had no alternative but to press on through, rather than attempt to climb out of it, thus using even more fuel.

A-Able was now tossed about unmercifully in the powerful air-currents and unaware of the extent of the damage already sustained, we could only hope that she could take it. The wind roaring through the aircraft became even more cutting and all thoughts of a safe return began to recede into the distance.

It was unlikely that fighters would operate in these conditions, but the returning bombers, blown off course, would be spread over a huge area, thus attracting radar predicted flak. We droned on, comforted by the steady roar of the engines during the interminable last few hours, and when Nobby called to announce a drop in wind speed, hopes again rose. At last in the dawn light I could see the dim outline of the channel coast, and hope was renewed as we watched the misty sunrise we had never dared to expect. The long night was at last at an end.

We were now very short of fuel, just willing the aircraft on, when Lewie decided we could not make base and began to call "DARKY-DARKY!" The coast of England lay shrouded under a layer of fog, dashing our hopes once more as we throttled back and began to lose height. With I.F.F. on 'DISTRESS' we were homing on 'Gee' when Tangmere called up and we realised we were almost 100 miles off track.

We were given a course and time to touch-down. There were others ahead in the queue, perhaps in worse condition, having lost an engine or undercarriage.

Tangmere, although a fighter base well known from 'Battle of Britain' days, was tonight acting as a 'lame ducks' aerodrome and with visibility suddenly down to zero, had become the last hope of many shattered bomber crews.

Lewie lowered the undercarriage, and it was with audible relief that we heard the thud of the locks, with the welcome green lights in the cockpit. We came in low over the sea, flaps down, just off Selsey Bill, straight on to the end of the runway. It was now almost daylight, though we were shrouded in mist. On landing, there was the sudden discovery that we had no brakes.

Running alongside and quickly to be overtaken was an R.A.F. van, on the back of which were the words 'FOLLOW ME' in green lights. As we gradually slowed, he managed once again to draw alongside, only to display 'STOP' in red lights.

We had no hope of stopping, and as sundry fuel-dumps hove out of the mist ahead, Lewie gave A-Able full rudder and we slewed off into the rough grass which finally brought us to a welcome halt. How the undercarriage was not wiped off, we never discovered, but the Halifax was a strong aircraft, for which we were forever grateful.

The ambulance drew up, and Ted was dispatched to hospital, full of metal and perspex, thoroughly shaken, but not we hoped, seriously injured.

Around us stood the now silent remnants of once brave aircraft and it was with no hint of surprise that the intelligence officer received our views of the night's work. Exhausted, we were put on the London train, a compartment to ourselves, and transported back to Snaith.

Chapter 5

A sense of loss and depression now fell upon us - we were no longer infallible. We talked cautiously about the immediate future and the possibility of leave. "They can't give the whole ruddy air-force a week's leave," complained Nobby.

"No, but they might give it to those who've lost their aircraft," replied Lewie. And then we began to think of A-Able never to fly again, unless rebuilt or used as spares for other 'Halibags'.

Back at Snaith, it was evident that the squadron had sustained serious losses. Apart from ourselves and others who had landed away with written-off aircraft, six crews had not returned and the mess seemed decimated. The total loss amounted to 96 aircraft - 672 men.

Despite the bad news, and the fact that no leave was forthcoming, life was for the living, and with glasses being raised to those who had gone, great quantities of beer were consumed. Our Skipper was then awarded an immediate commission and the D.F.C., which he richly deserved, but the crew received not a mention. At the time it was a hard fact to swallow for those of us who had all been through the mill together on that appalling night. Strangely, we felt depressed not having an aircraft to call our own when others were so busy. Borrowing the first available bicycle, I cycled over to Burn, some ten miles distant, to see Eleanor, now installed in her new post. We met in the village, and after a supper of the interminable baked beans, the only food readily available in out of the way places, we repaired to the pub. It appeared that Burn also had received severe losses, and after a few drinks, Eleanor turned to me and said, "You look very tired. Are you sleeping properly?" and I had to admit that we all had great difficulty in shutting off our minds, and were probably nearing the end of our tether.

"How many trips have you got to go?" she asked.

"Four or five," I replied, unwilling to mention the definite number.

"Tell me about it," she said. "I heard that you'd landed at Tangmere. Were you shot-up, or short of fuel?"

"Both," I replied, and went on briefly to describe the experience, its horrors, and the devastating sight of so many stricken bombers, our hopes and fears as the interminable night dragged on. She remained silent, and clung to me as we left the pub and went out into the now rain drenched night.

Collecting my bicycle, we stood close in the pouring rain. "Promise me you'll write to my mother if..." I was quite unable to finish the sentence. It was an emotionally charged moment, the rain forgotten, before Eleanor recovered and was able to whisper her answer.

Minutes later she said, "You can't ride back in this weather, you'll get soaked."

To which I replied, "I could probably sleep in a 'Halibag', there are plenty around."

"No," she replied. "You can have Jean's bed. We share a billet and she's on duty tonight."

So it was decided, and I found myself once again 'out of bounds'.

In the grey light of the morning, a knock and sudden shout, "Eight o'clock sergeant!" brought me to consciousness. Eleanor's reply, "Thank you corporal," with finger to her lips, only just prevented my own automatic response. It was with silent amusement that we gathered my things together and I prepared to depart while the going was good and before Jean returned from duty.

Retrieving my bicycle from the hedge behind the 'Waafery', I bolted off down the long bare concrete track to the road. Racing past the guard hut, hoping not to be noticed, I received a somewhat startled wave, but pressed on at high speed to escape to the public highway.

Two days later a brand new Halifax skimmed over the hedge, to land with a whisper. We were admiring this new bomber with the latest extended wings, quite sure that it was to replace the lost A-Able, when out stepped a single W.A.A.F. officer. She was a member of the Air Transport Auxiliary, the first we had seen, and we were greatly impressed, knowing full well that the 'Halibag' was a heavy aircraft to handle, particularly on approach and landing, with so many things to do at the last moment.

Orders soon came through that we were to air-test the new arrival, particularly with a view to the flying characteristics with the additional wing area.

She was superb, quietly gleaming in her new colours and squadron marking, now with a wing span of 103 feet. "Now we shall be up with the Lancs at last," announced Nobby. "With the extra lift we shall be able to drop our bombs on somebody else for a change!" We all knew what he meant, but Lewie, now resplendent with his new rings and 'gong', reminded us that we would still have to fly at heights given at briefing, whatever they might be.

There was now an unexpected lull in operations, due we felt sure, to the fact that the hierarchy had at last realised that they were asking too much of bomber-crews and were loath to lay on another long range attack in the shortening days.

In the interval, we took on a new engineer and flew A-Able whenever possible, revelling in her new smell, as yet untainted by leaking hydraulic oil and fuel.

And then, at a stroke everything changed. Our efforts were transferred to a new type of attack, this time on small targets in France and Belgium, railway yards, ammunition dumps and armament factories, using smaller numbers of aircraft actually controlled over the target by P.F.F. air to air on R.T. Briefing was exciting. We were to bomb the railway yards at Lille, at 7000 feet, low level for us, and listen out for the master bomber's instructions.

Armed with a maximum load of H.E. bombs and incendiaries, now that fuel capacity was no longer a prime factor, we took off on the shortest 'trip' we had ever made. "A piece of cake!" cheerful voices had shouted as we left the briefing room, and so it proved to be.

It was full moon and clear as the French coast appeared and there ahead was the target already being illuminated by the Pathfinder flares, interspersed with the inevitable flak. As we approached, the first green markers burst into brilliant bright light, and there was a fair amount of excited chat in A-Able, until the voice of the master of ceremonies, loud and clear, exhorted the main force to, "bomb on the greens - bomb on the greens!"

Timing was of acute importance because otherwise, 200 plus bombers could not possibly pass over this one small spot all within the space of 10 minutes. As it was, there was a feverish jockeying for position and both gunners were busy giving Lewie a running commentary on the ever-changing position of our fellows, none wanting to give way and risk going round again in the increasing flak.

Calling, 'Bomb doors open," and checking everything in readiness, I studied the quickly approaching target below which, from our new low height, stood out sharp and clear, a vast change from our recent operations.

Shining in the moonlight the snaking railway lines came in from all points to converge at the centre of the aiming point, which was already being reinforced by further markers. The M.C. called again over the R.T., encouraging us ever onwards. I could imagine him in the Mosquito clearly visible below, flying almost at ground level, flitting to and fro across the engine sheds on the edge of the complicated junction.

In a haze of daunting tracer, at first lazily rising, to accelerate rapidly into a shower of golden balls, Lewie eased A-Able over as I called, "Right steady-Right," determined to hit this perfectly defined spot despite the buffeting. Photo flashes were going off all round us as I called "Bombs gone," and Lewie held her on course until our own flash had coincided with the camera. This was something worth photographing, and I watched as our string of HEs flew over the ground to erupt close to the engine sheds. It was an exhilarating experience, just what we imagined pin-point bombing should be like, and as Lewie closed the bomb-doors we turned for home.

The distant voice of the master bomber calling, "Well done main force. You can go home now!" rounded off a perfect trip and we were home within the hour.

We were in high spirits at the de-briefing, and reinforced by the coffee and rum, gave glowing accounts of the ideal in and out operation. "If we get some more of these short trips," suggested Nobby, "we stand a good chance of finishing a tour."

"Yes, but you know 'Jerry'," answered Lewie, "this was the first one, and we took him unawares. As soon as he catches on, he'll transfer more fighters to France."

It did not enter our heads that these railway targets might be the prelude to the much talked about invasion.

Next morning, early for us, we hurried to the intelligence room, eager to inspect and compare the bombing photos, delighted to find ours among the best examples.

There was a renewed spirit in the mess that evening. Everyone believed the tide had turned and drank heavily to a future which had so far eluded them.

It was now April, and the countryside reflected the first flush of spring as the new lambs appeared on the Yorkshire hills, and the overall drab greyness gave way to green. Seen in daylight at low level on our frequent test flights, it was brought home to us that in our ever changing world, these hills had remained constant through a thousand years, altered only by the seasons. We were beginning to enjoy life again with the lengthening days, and towards the end of the month were briefed to fly once more to France.

The target was the large railway junction at Villeneuve-St-Georges, south of Paris, and A-Able rose eagerly into clear skies lit by a pale moon. We had been warned at briefing to bomb only as directed by the master bomber and that the city itself was on no account to be attacked.

Crossing the enemy coast at 7000 feet, the usual searchlights and flak awaited us, and at our low height seemed particularly venomous, but we were soon through and heading for the outskirts of Paris, where the outer defences clearly marked the size of the city. To the south, all was light and colour, the first green markers sparkling merrily, with P.F.F flares overhead. With bomb-doors open on our run-in, a sudden call from the master bomber far below caused a last minute panic. "Ignore the greens, main force, ignore the greens....! Bomb on the reds! Bomb on the reds!" at which point a cluster of reds appeared as if by magic upwind of the greens and we immediately swung on with only seconds to spare.

Concentrating on the reds, my vision was suddenly broken by the huge black shadow of a Halifax passing immediately below, a mere second before I pressed the tit. It was with relief that I watched the bombs on their way, knowing that it was clear.

As we left the target with the master bomber's voice ringing in our ears, "Well done main force. Off you go!" we congratulated ourselves on yet another satisfactory result in this new type of pin-point bombing.

The return trip was uneventful, but near the French coast a series of blue lights moving rapidly below attracted my attention, as they were obviously airborne and yet did not appear to be going in any definite direction. Perhaps they were the new flying bombs. No doubt the intelligence officer would know, and at debriefing I described the strange sightings and we were told that they were most probably caused by the exhaust stream of the new jet-engine fighters the Germans were known to be developing.

Undisturbed by this news, we fell into bed, confident of a good aiming point picture when the 'ops' photos came in next day.

At lunch time, secretly delighted with our results, we decided this deserved some small celebration to include the ground crew who had done so much to keep A-Able on the top line. Arrangements were well in hand when all plans were hastily dashed by the booming of the Tannoy. Ops were on again. The party would have to be postponed.

Another railway yard, at Montzen near Aachen was the target, and we were detailed for the second wave in a total of 144 bombers. Mosquitos would be dropping target indicators and the whole affair would be controlled by the master bomber as before.

Amid a cloud of winking navigation lights, we climbed over England to our operating height of 7000 feet, and having already doused lights, passed over the Thames Estuary.

Crossing the Dutch coast there was no flak. All was suspiciously quiet and Lewie called up the gunners to keep a look out, as there were already ominous glows in the sky ahead. We were some fifteen miles from the target when we were hit.

We never saw the fighter, if fighter it was, but A-Able shuddered violently under the onslaught, and immediately we were on fire in the port inner engine, close to the fuel tanks. Lewie jabbed the fire extinguisher buttons but without effect. Behind us streamed a cloud of burning petrol, and we knew we had finally had it.

Parachutes were quickly clipped on even before Lewie called, "Parachutes on chaps," and a few seconds later the shout, "Bale out- Bale out!" galvanised us into action.

The wing was now burning furiously. The escape drill, etched into my mind during every previous trip, now sprang into action.

Lifting the escape hatch under my bombing position, and battling with the roaring wind, I dropped it through the hole, and as Nobby and Mac passed me on their way out, I returned to give Lewie his parachute from the stowage position. He waved me away and motioned me to get out and at that split second the wing exploded and we turned over.

Chapter 6

I found myself in the air without fear and in total darkness, the silence absolute. A deep feeling of calm overcame me, and I felt cradled in a great stillness. I seemed to be in another world. It was only when I discovered my parachute and pulled the D-ring that fear returned, as with a deafening crack the chute flashed by my face and I seemed suddenly borne upwards at high speed as it broke my downward plunge.

But I was still falling and below me was the wide expanse of the River Maas. Thoughts flashed through my mind of a dimly remembered parachute drill of how to change direction in the air, and this had some effect. I did not relish the idea of finishing up in the 'drink'. The appalling realisation that one life was over and that I was now falling into the hands of the enemy was somewhat lessened by the apparent ploughed fields visible below, shining in the moonlight.

Plans for escape filled my mind. I was falling into open countryside, they would never find me.

Seconds later, trees flashed by me and I crashed into a factory roof up to my knees in tiles, smashing my nose on the roof ridge. The huge white parachute hung above, suspended from a tall chimney, advertising my presence.

The silence was broken by shouts and the sound of running feet as Dutchmen suddenly appeared to clamber up the drain pipes to release me from my trap.

Climbing down over their backs, glad to be on solid ground again, they escorted me to a nearby house, where within seconds I was surrounded by smiling faces.

The house soon became full to bursting. Cigarettes and drinks were thrust upon me and amid the interminable shaking of hands, excited voices shouted, "When is the invasion - when is the invasion?"

"Soon," I answered, "very soon!" little knowing when it might be. I knew no more than they.

I was then officially captured, when the local German army appeared in the shape of a little old man who announced, "For you the war is over!" and I was put into a waiting car. During the short car ride, suddenly realising that I had not had time to dispose of my so far 'secret' bombing orders, I managed to tear them up and drop them out of the car window which was very fortunately open. I did not wish the enemy to have any more information than they already had.

On entering the local police station I was able to surreptitiously throw the remains behind a large shrub adjacent to the doorway and I felt relatively happy that they had nothing on me. I knew that interrogation would follow.

The sight that met my eyes caused me to smile with joy and relief. Seated on a stool in one of the cells was Rebel, the mid-upper gunner. He had sustained a slight head wound and with a bandage surrounding his head pushing up a great quiff of black hair, he looked like a Red Indian chief which, with his high cheek bones, denoted his undoubted ancestry.

No news was available on any other members of our crew, but I felt sure that Nobby and Mac should have made it, unless they had been caught up in the explosion. The fact that they were not with us was bad news. We now learnt that we were in Maastricht and together, escorted by two guards, we were taken to the railway station.

On the way through Holland, to where we knew not, we were able to talk, and Rebel's escape appeared no less miraculous than my own. As he had been climbing down from the turret to make his way to the rear escape hatch, the broken wing sliced off the end of the fuselage and he was wafted out of the large hole thus created.

We had little idea of what was going to happen to us, but we were grateful to be alive, and watched with interest when we stopped at various railway stations, the antics of the ill-fed labour force working on the railway lines. Upon recognising us, they had probably seen many R.A.F. on the same route to the prison camps, they immediately stopped work and jammed their long crowbars into the ground to form the obvious 'V' for victory sign. It was a mute signal to their only hope of freedom, that same freedom which now applied to ourselves. We had a lot in common, though their hardship had lasted for years.

The train rattled on through Venlo and Eindhoven, where we were amazed to see the Philips radio factory emblazoned with signs and advertising all in English, though under the iron hand of the enemy. We were later transferred to another train, again with the hard wooden slatted seats, the two guards sitting on the outside so that we had the window seats, where we were able to pass the time watching the countryside flash by.

The train was packed with German troops, armed to the teeth and we began to feel a little nervous as we passed the remains of Düsseldorf and Cologne, once great cities which we had helped to destroy. Littered streets, and the shells of roofless buildings met our gaze as far as one could see, and we were glad that London had not received the same annihilation. It was a sorry sight, but we felt a certain pride that the R.A.F. was the only force able to carry the war to the enemy at this time, and that with the evident destruction of the heart of Germany, the war, if not won, had no doubt been shortened.

We travelled the length of the Rhine Valley, now clothed in the beautiful pink blossom of almond and cherry on the sloping hillsides, with the huge river meandering below and I thought with all this, why do the Germans want more? Perhaps it was only Hitler and his generals.

And then we arrived at Frankfurt, to which we had been several times before, though in another life. Frankfurt was the main collecting point for the R.A.F. prisoners of war, and with the usual German thoroughness we were to go straight into solitary confinement.

It is difficult to describe the effect of solitary confinement under these conditions. To be pitched into a cell with little light from the high window, with only one's thoughts for company for days on end is a soul destroying experience. With the future uncertain and the stark horror of losing most of one's friends still uppermost in the mind, a state of shock occurs when the body shakes and teeth rattle involuntarily. Thoughts of how one came to be in this degrading position press upon a mind already in turmoil. My parents would not know if I was alive or dead - I would be posted missing - and yet I was alive. It would be months before they knew. Eleanor would immediately know that our aircraft had failed to return, and our last conversation filled my mind.

For two days I could not stomach the meagre food offered, but this was the whole idea of 'solitary', to break one down to the state of mind where any human contact would be welcome and the prisoner would be only too glad to answer all questions at the interrogation to come. After three days the interrogations started in earnest and took the form of two hourly sessions twice a day, first with a very pleasant

German major followed by an SS type officer who harangued and blustered in the hope of extracting information about our aircraft and our squadron.

Cups of tea and cigarettes were offered, questions were asked, "Where did you live, where did you go to school?" all these queries finally building to the really important questions to which they required answers.

Bogus Red Cross forms were thrust across the table to be filled in, with the threat that if uncompleted the Red Cross would be unable to make up their P.O.W. lists, and therefore no one would know of my existence.

I was forced to repeat ad nauseam that the Red Cross did not need to know my home address, squadron number or type of aircraft. All that they required were my name, rank and number, and of this I was confident, at which the German interrogator, speaking excellent English returned me to stew in my cell.

This went on for a further five days of halting conversations, coming to an abrupt end on my part when service matters were raised. It became a battle of wits, but I knew that with no doubt more P.O.W.s arriving daily, my incarceration could not last forever.

I thought again of my escape from the aircraft. My last recollection was of standing opposite Lewie in the act of giving him his parachute. When he waved me away, I was still some ten feet from the escape hatch when the aircraft blew up. I could not fathom it, it was a miracle, and then to be able to recover consciousness in time to pull the rip-cord.

I knew that Lewie had gone down with the aircraft. He was one of that gallant band who were to give their lives for their crews.

The interminable interrogations went on daily and at last the German officer in an exasperated mood asked, "Do you not want to join your comrades in the main compound? They have good food and pleasant quarters."

I had no means of knowing whether this promise was true or false, but I did want to join Rebel, my one friend, before he was perhaps sent off to a P.O.W. camp without me. I asked again for news of the rest of the crew but obtained no satisfactory answer.

After ten days inside, I was at last released from confinement to join the others free to wander the huge main area, to converse at last with my own kind.

It was good to be open to the sky again, to feel and breathe fresh air. It was early May and Rebel and I enjoyed the spring sunshine as we strolled the well worn path beaten smooth by the feet of countless P.O.W.s close to the perimeter wire, searching for faces which we might recognise from an earlier life, but there were none. All were strangers, but not for long as friendships were struck and strange tales were told of crazy escapes, still fresh in the mind. A tall rangy New Zealander described how he had hit the ground head-first with his parachute harness entangled round his ankles. Unknown to him his harness had been partially shot away and upon pulling the rip-cord, the whole affair had slipped down his body fortunately to catch round his feet, to deposit him upside down.

It was a happy yet sad time. Some of our fellows had been badly burned, which was not surprising, but to witness the actual effects at close quarters was something of a shock. Some had no hair and were gravely disfigured with eyes puffed up and closed being led about by their friends. Others had hands and feet bound up, testimony to unseen horrors. Rebel had been more fortunate; his head was healing well, and I could breathe through my nose so presumed all was well. All I had was an enormous black bruise now turning to yellow on my lower chest where the parachute harness had impinged upon hitting the factory roof. We spoke again of our own good fortune and wondered afresh why we were the only two to escape, feeling almost a sense of guilt that we had been spared.

And then started the great exodus to our final camp. We were marched in a straggling formation down to a nearby rail yard surrounded by guards with fearsome looking black Alsatians at heel.

With much shouting and gesticulating on the part of the Germans, and answering shouts of "Get stuffed!" from ourselves we slowly climbed aboard the closed cattle trucks, already learning how far we could go in annoying the enemy.

Each cattle truck was supposed to hold about fifty men though we could not all lay down together. The four windows were covered with barbed wire and there was a thin layer of straw on the floor. The great sliding doors were at last shut and bolted, and the long train set off with much banging and shunting.

We had no idea where we were going or how long it would take. Twice a day, morning and evening, the train would stop, when guards came along handing out slops and hunks of bread, and at these times we were allowed to jump down on the tracks to relieve ourselves, but as the journey progressed this became less of a need, and just an excuse for exercise. The nights were very cold and we were glad it was not winter time, which would have been unbearable. The journey lasted eight days, and at the end it was with undisguised relief that we were on the march again to a camp deep in the forest near Heyderkrug in East Prussia, a distance of nearly one thousand miles traversed in indescribable discomfort.

The camp was well established and many nationalities seemed to be present in separate large compounds spread over a considerable area.

At regular intervals around the perimeter fence were the 'goon' boxes, tall wooden structures which housed two goons (German guards were always know as goons), equipped with mounted machine guns and searchlights - were we never to get away from searchlights? As our motley throng began to fill the fore-lager, eager faces pressed against the adjoining wire, keen to spy out and welcome any long lost friends from a previous life, stretching right back to training days. It was rather like being in a zoo, and we were all well aware of our now sloppy appearance and heavily bearded faces.

Harassed with shouts and loud Germanic curses, we were divided up and escorted to the inner compound in groups of a hundred to be allotted our huts. These huts stood on stilts, well clear of the ground so that guard dogs could pass underneath and so sniff out any attempts at the ever present pastime of tunnelling.

Inside were rows of double bunks, with here and there a rough table, and Rebel and I made our choice, he on a top bunk and myself underneath. Conditions were austere in the extreme; each bed was equipped with about nine narrow slats supporting a straw filled palliasse of uncertain heritage.

Twice a day we were to be called out on 'appel', the obligatory roll-call, when in four ranks we were lined up to be counted fore and aft by two 'goons', who then reported to the camp Commandant, a lengthy procedure often exacerbated by our pretended inability to understand what was required of us. It all helped to pass the time, of which we had plenty. Also on parade was the senior R.A.F. officer to whom we were directly responsible, though happily there was no 'bull' in the camp and we did no useful work. The time was spent reading books supplied from the Red Cross library, an invaluable institution entirely run by the inmates, who issued other useful adjuncts from that marvellous society such as drawing books and pencils and paper.

Walking the circuit was the chief form of activity, taking care not to overstep the trip wire, positioned some eight feet from the main perimeter fence, permission having to be granted from the nearest 'goon-box' to retrieve any lost balls, otherwise one was likely to be shot at in this 'verboten' area. Outside the main fence, topped by a mass of barbed wire was a cleared area of thirty yards before the real forest commenced, just in case anyone attempted escape which was virtually impossible as the 'goon-boxes' each swept a carefully controlled section. The forest was beautiful, with tall pines littered with cones and the pale new green shoots of the larch breaking through last year's timber. Inside, the camp was a desert of well trodden sand, beaten down by thousands of feet, except where a small garden sprang up thanks to a timely gift of seeds again from the Red Cross.

The Germans always placed their P.O.W. camps on sandy soil, thus making it very difficult to carry out satisfactory tunnelling, and blue overalled 'goons' were regularly to be seen prodding certain suspect areas of ground with long metal spikes searching for the elusive tunnel. There was always a tunnel under construction somewhere, but very few were privy to its position or progress.

The atmosphere of the camp was in some respects like an English village. There was a C of E church, a barber's shop, a home made theatre, a musical society and a proper shop where mainly food items were available at a price. The Red Cross made this possible by sending individual food parcels which included cigarettes and tobacco, which at this stage arrived fairly frequently. As the German issue of these essentials was so meagre, visits to the shop became frequent so long as one had the necessary currency; cigarettes.

Each day, prices were listed of the various items on offer, and if any item was in short supply this was reflected in the price, rather like the Stock Exchange. It was a wonderful system and if one was well established and had plenty of fags, the living was good. To the newcomer like ourselves there was a time lag before one received a parcel and was able to enter the market.

All these establishments were run entirely by the prisoners for the prisoners. The Jerry guards did not normally bother us unless we bothered them, though we considered it our duty to do so on every possible occasion.

As dusk fell, the compound gates were closed and barred, the perimeter lights came on and searchlights began their regular traversing of the rows of huts, and anyone surprised outside after this time was likely to be attacked by one or more of the large Alsatian dogs released into the compound.

It became a favourite pastime of ours as the night progressed, to attract one of the dogs with a biscuit, to a position under a window where he was immediately belaboured with a handy broom stick to go howling off into the night. This was a source of great amusement and a great trial to the Jerries who would perforce have to turn out from their comfortable billets to check the disturbance. Those on duty at night had no peace until they occasionally withdrew the dogs, and we were able to make a dash across to the opposite hut and so add a little spice to life.

During the day Rebel and I roamed the three other large compounds still eager to search out a known face, but with the thousands roaming about, this became a virtual impossibility. Ball games of all sorts were in progress and here and there one came across budding musicians practising on their much prized instruments, obviously sent out from home. These were no doubt inmates of long standing, some of whom had even sent for their 'best blue'. This they wore proudly on roll calls just to be different from the rest of us who dressed in whatever came to hand, largely swaps from the Red Cross, who also supplied great-coats, gifts from a variety of nations in all colours.

In cold weather, roll calls were quite a colourful occasion, and as these great-coats served also as virtually our only blanket they were greatly prized and guarded.

The ablutions were primitive in the extreme and generally open to the winds, so that clothing was only washed in fine weather and thus given a chance to dry before re-wearing. Anyone who had two or more sets of clothes was indeed fortunate, and only the most long standing inmates were in this happy position.

Frequent rumours sped like wild-fire through the camp. Russian P.O.W.s began to arrive in small numbers and were put in a separate compound where their sonorous voices could be heard singing songs of their homeland, their emaciated bodies clinging to the wire.

Secret wireless sets were in operation in the camp, put together from bits obtained from the 'goons' by nothing more than bribery and corruption. It would start with a few cigarettes or a packet of butter or chocolate and the 'goons', were trapped. There was no shortage of the skills required to assemble a simple yet efficient wireless, as there were many wireless operator P.O.W.s only too glad to exercise their cunning to tune into the B.B.C.'s world service.

News of the long promised invasion spread by word of mouth and although few details were known, there was a new spirit in the camp, and we walked tall, knowing that we knew something of which the average 'goon' was in complete ignorance. We now began to spread alarm and despondency among the Jerries with whom we had daily contact, assuring them that if they treated us well we might be prepared to think kindly of them when the end came. It was now our turn to shout, "For you the war is over!", but it was evident from the reaction of some of the older men set to guard us, that as far as they were concerned the end could not come soon enough. They were, no doubt, underfed and thoroughly bored with their job, but with the younger soldiers it was a different matter. Of a different breed and still imbued with the spirit of the master race having risen from the ranks of the Hitler Youth, they were arrogant and strutting, rather like the S.S. who made occasional visits in their long black leather coats and black hats.

From time to time there would be a purge, when we would all be shut out of our huts for long periods while the 'goons' searched for any tools or implements which might be used for improper purposes. They rarely found anything because we had become adept at concealing our treasured tools, but if such were found, the particular hut involved would have no lights for a week or some similar punishment. There were always reprisals for any misdemeanour. We asked for trouble and suffered it gladly when it came. Any departure from the usual camp routine was welcome and to be encouraged.

We had not been long at Heyderkrug, when word went round that we were to move to another camp, though no details were forthcoming. Rumour had it that "The 'Russkies' were coming," and that rather than lose their prisoners, the Jerries would in all probability move us westward.

The camp became a bee-hive with inmates running from hut to hut shouting "The 'Russkies' are coming, the 'Russkies' are coming!", everyone being delighted at the obvious embarrassment of the Jerries who knew little more than ourselves.

We had received virtually no news of the Russian offensive and it was a surprise to us, but as we had already heard dire tales of the treatment meted out by that nation we were only too happy to stay with the Germans and retreat with them.

Collecting together our few treasured possessions, we were once again on the march to the nearest railway line where the cattle trucks stood waiting, deep in the forest.

We were sorry to leave such a long established well run camp, but sensing that the war was now moving in our favour, felt that it was only a question of time before the armies met in the middle, and we would be finally released.

Apart from ourselves, one end of the train seemed packed with women and children, no doubt also keen to get out of the path of the feared 'Russkies', though their final destination was even more uncertain than our own.

After three days of cramped conditions and little food we fell out of the cattle trucks to form up and make the long march to the new camp on the outskirts of Thorn in Poland. We were wearing our treasured great-coats, not wishing to leave them behind, and with our only belongings slung over our shoulders we were stifled in the summer heat. Surrounded on all sides by the sounds of the clattering equipment of the Jerry guards with their silently slinking but ever alert Alsatians we stumbled on.

After some miles a shower of summer rain refreshed us and we were quick to suck the lapels of our great-coats to extract the excess moisture in order to slake our parched throats. We had drunk little fluid for three days, and had become seriously dehydrated.

Thorn appeared to be more of a transit camp with few amenities, and the P.O.W.s set to work erecting various buildings for common use with the materials on site, some offered, some purloined from the Jerries.

It was now early summer and very hot on the vast sandy plain taken up by the four compounds of the camp, with hardly a tree in sight and almost none in the camp itself, which was built on virgin heathland in the middle of nowhere.

Among the constructional improvements carried out by the P.O.W.s was an ingenious shower arrangement whereby upon pulling a string a large quantity of water was released upon one's head, to disappear immediately into the sand beneath. This contraption was very popular and queues formed in the heat of the day to take advantage of this innovation. The Jerries seemed unperturbed by the vast quantities of water consumed by this system, but as less water was consequently used from other outlets perhaps it made little difference. As it was, many inmates washed their clothes 'in situ' while wearing them, and then passed under the showers to sluice themselves off before drying them while taking the daily exercise on the circuit.

This edifice soon became a meeting point for P.O.W.s, as word went around, rather like the well of ancient days.

Not far from the camp was a German fighter base, audible to our trained ears when the wind was in the right direction, and the fighter pilots, no doubt hearing of our previous airborne exploits took great pleasure in strafing us on every possible occasion. Messerschmitt 109s tore across the bare heath, at low level between the 'goon-boxes' causing one to duck down and almost to take cover. We never quite got used to the experience and as one bright spark put it, "They only have to push the button and they could release all the Jerries guards for the front line!" and no one with certainty could deny the possibility, now that the Fatherland was under pressure from all sides.

Life in the camp was gradually becoming much harder. The food parcels which we had relied upon were now arriving erratically and we learnt that some sealed wagons had been broken into and the contents stolen. The Germans were also getting hungry, and this was reflected in the daily issue we now received in the camp. Our rations were now down to a quarter of a loaf of rye bread and a bowl of soup, twice a day, with a cup of acorn coffee. The soup consisted of a watery gruel which might contain, if one were lucky, a couple of small potatoes and a lump of meat or gristle. Everyone swore that the meat was basically of the horse variety, but as it had been stewed for so long, it was generally quite tender and much prized. The days were hot, and the interior of the huts stifling, and at night the residual heat together with the added heat of the hundred bodies became almost unbearable even with the few available windows open.

Most of the inmates were glad when it rained except for the select few actually involved in a tunnelling operation. Rain was the bugbear of these underground operators as excess water drained down to weaken the roof of the tunnel which had then to be shored up, using the only wood close at hand, which accounted for certain huts to be remarkably short of bed boards to support their palliasses.

This fact did not go unnoticed by the Jerries, and the 'goons' were soon despatched to prod the adjacent surroundings with their long spikes. When the 'goons' were engrossed in this activity, a small crowd would inevitably collect, and those with a little knowledge of the language though fully aware of the reason, would politely enquire as to the object of the exercise, whereupon the 'goon' involved in this unrewarding occupation, unable to give a satisfactory answer, would invariably move on to pastures new.

Whichever hut one entered, the inmates seemed to be involved in escape talk, though few schemes were carried through and we never heard of a successful escape. The attraction was the close proximity of the River Vistula, on which huge barges sailed all the way to Danzig, a distance of some eighty miles, probably captained by Poles who might be friendly. Once in the port of Danzig it was considered feasible that one could stowaway in a ship going to neutral Sweden. All the variables were discussed at length, but always the most difficult part of the operation was the escape from the camp itself. All escape plans were then suddenly shelved; we were to move again. Rumours spread through the camp that the 'Russkies' were still coming and that we were to be transported into Germany.

Chapter 7

Once again on the long march to the railway line, we were glad for the change of scene and the apparent freedom of not being surrounded by miles of wire, though the chances of escape were nil with so many armed guards and their even more feared dogs. The surrounding countryside consisted of low scrub as far as one could see, affording little cover, and no one felt inclined to risk a bullet or a pack of dogs.

Remembering our earlier forced march, we had now equipped ourselves with a supply of water carried in containers of all descriptions; enough we hoped to see us through the long train journey.

The cattle trucks intended for our use were in an indescribable condition. We could only imagine the state of the previous inmates, and in a body we refused to enter them until promised an issue of fresh straw from a nearby farm, to which we were despatched under guard. Having kicked out all the foul straw onto the railway line we condescended to jump aboard with our fresh supply of straw, glad once again to have shown our strength of will in the face of the enemy, though with very good reason.

With the sliding doors once again locked and barred and with faces peering out of barbed-wire windows, we clanged and banged our way westwards, confident that at least we were now going towards our own troops.

Twice a day when the train stopped, we looked forward to our wander up and down the tracks and the chance to stretch our legs. The food was of almost secondary importance, being the usual hunk of dry rye bread and a mess of red cabbage or foul sauerkraut, which we ate only to keep alive.

There was always a great hubbub with much cursing and shouting as the Jerry guards attempted to push and prod us back into the trucks when the engine whistled its final warning. There was often an element of 'last aboard the train' which roused the Jerries to fury, much to our delight.

It was five days before we reached our destination and some swore that they would never get into a cattle truck again whatever the outcome.

Another long march took us to Stalag 357 at Fallingbostell on Luneburg Heath, where many other prisoners had already been transferred from other camps. This camp covered a large area with several huge compounds emanating from a central fore-lager, which housed some Jerry billets and several storerooms, from which we drew our palliasses and anything else the camp had to offer, which was not very much.

Again, a mass of faces greeted us, searching for long lost friends, and occasionally one heard the shout of delighted recognition as someone picked out a figure long forgotten and given up for dead.

Rebel and I, as soon as we had bagged a couple of bunks in the hut allocated to our intake, were soon off on a 'recce' of our surroundings, first remembering the number and position of our hut, as there were rows and rows of identical buildings all raised off the ground on stilt-like legs.

All three services seemed to be present in varying numbers, each within their own compound open to all during the day, but the majority were R.A.F., those who had been lucky enough to have saved their lives on the end of a parachute during the previous four years of operations. It was a pitifully small percentage of the huge numbers of men involved during that period and complete crews were rarely to be found.

But there was a good spirit in the camp and church services in the beautifully kept church were regularly attended, as was the Red Cross library run by the inmates, who also kept a small but valuable supply of the necessary drawing books, and pencils and paper. Many 'Kriegies' were to be found committing their thoughts and memories to paper and almost everyone had a drawing or two to offer, many of whom had never had the time or opportunity to test their talents before. So the time was not entirely wasted and indeed many of the long serving members had received professional text books from home and were deeply involved in the basics of architecture and accountancy.

Any in depth inspection of a new camp always included the ablutions and, of necessity, the latrines. The ablutions consisted of the usual open sided affair with long wooden troughs fed by taps suspended above, many of which through age and ill use failed to respond to their handles.

The latrines were remarkable if judged only by their size. Perhaps a hundred yards long, with a hundred holes to suit, they were covered but open to the wire and forest beyond, a truly delightful view which was very peaceful and thought provoking.

From time to time, to add interest to the proceedings, a lighted bunch of paper would be surreptitiously dropped into the first hole by the perpetrators of this dastardly deed, who would watch with fascination as each inmate in turn jumped up in alarm as the flaming torch floated down to the end of the line. So great was the length of the edifice that few inmates had any warning of the conflagration bearing down upon them and the resulting confusion was a joy to behold. Such were the tricks played upon one another to brighten the day, and this was one that never failed to bring the desired result.

As the year progressed the daily rations were cut yet again, to one slice of rye bread a day plus the usual issue of soup, and to ensure fairness we divided ourselves into groups of ten, and then the loaf was cut into ten pieces by one of our members and lots were cast as to which slice was allotted to each member of the group. This ritual was to become an important highlight of the day and its observance was obligatory.

Red Cross parcels arrived rarely and an issue of a quarter parcel was much prized, particularly if it contained a tin of 'Klim', an excellent powdered milk, the container of which could be beaten into plates and formed into implements with the few tools at our disposal. 'Klim' tins were also used to build clever contraptions for quick 'brewing-up'. Based on the idea of the forge, a forced draught was obtained by a hand made fan actuated by a crank handle through the end of a round 'Klim' tin. This forced a blast of air into a secondary chamber under the pot to be boiled. In this chamber, odd bits of paper and torn up boxes could be quickly brought to a glowing mass thus boiling the pot in quick time using the minimum of materials. It was yet another example of the ingenuity brought into use by men with time on their hands and the demands of the moment.

At this time there were at least three wireless sets in the camp, sometimes concealed in musical instruments and we received regular accounts of the course of the war, and in particular the progress of the invasion, which filled us with glee as the average Jerry knew nothing of these exciting happenings.

Every day a news reader was to be seen going the rounds of the huts giving the latest news in some detail from a prepared sheet, and on arrival at each hut a watch was set up at doors and windows to check for wandering 'goons'.

At the approach of the enemy, the call "Goons up!" would pass down the hut and the tense silence of the avidly listening audience would immediately revert to the usual hubbub of hut life until the snooper had passed on.

Rebel and I joined those involved in the upkeep of the camp garden and with our close bed fellows Buzz and Mike we enjoyed many pleasant hours in this oasis amongst the desert of the compounds, planting the Red Cross issue of seeds unwanted by other 'Kriegies'.

It was a pleasant peaceful place, away from the incessant shouts of the football pitch and the crowded circuit of the compound where hundreds spent their day stomping round in a faint effort to keep fit despite the failing rations.

Regular forays began to be made at dusk to search the rear of the Jerry Kitchen quarters for the odd swede or turnip which were hastily gathered up before 'lock-up' when the compound main gates were closed and all the lights came on, ending all further searches.

Those with a carefully controlled hoard of cigarettes bartered with the Jerry guards for a loaf of bread or a packet of margarine, but there were some who offered cigarette packets which on inspection proved to be empty, which naturally infuriated the Jerries beyond measure, and there was nothing more rewarding than watching the gesticulations of a thoroughly incensed Jerry.

There was obviously a limit to our powers of harassing our captors but any excuse was gladly seized upon, and when the 'Yanks' overflew the camp in their tight formations on the way to their target, everyone turned out to parade in the centre of the compounds to shout and cheer them on their way. The Fortresses, first only visible by their vapour traits in the distance, came over in waves, and one could occasionally hear the rattle of machine-gun fire as they exchanged shots with the German fighters, constantly diving on them from all angles, leaving winding vapour trails which criss-crossed the deep blue sky.

It was an impressive sight which served to cheer us up for days, particularly when we were able to hear the results of their endeavours on the daily radio report. This was now appearing in a very limited edition in print which went the rounds of the huts, thus cutting down the risk to the to the news-reader, who if caught with the leaflet would no doubt be confined to 'solitary' for a week at least.

It never ceased to amaze us just what was going on in secret in the camp. The fact that the material required to make a small printing press had somehow been smuggled in, assembled and brought into regular daily use was beyond belief, and at some risk with so many 'ferrets' inspecting the huts at regular intervals.

The long evenings after 'lock-up', when the searchlights on the 'goon-boxes' swept the empty compound, was an opportunity for us to improve the art of dog-baiting, the much prized biscuits now being too valuable to offer the snarling beasts prowling under the huts. Each member of the hut now had a responsibility to search his soup daily and retrieve and carefully store any lump of inedible gristle which might be tied to a length of string and used as a bait. These baits were hung suspended above the head of the slavering Alsatian who would inevitably attempt to climb into the window, whereupon a surprise blow would achieve the desired effect and the resultant cacophony would wake the camp and turn out the guards. Sometimes it was possible to initiate a fight between two of the brutes with alarming consequences! We revelled in the disturbances caused and were fully prepared to accept any and all reprisals which might follow our simple pleasures.

After repeatedly responding to these alarms and excursions the Jerries finally reached the end of their tether and on morning roll call the inmates of our hut were kept on parade for an interminable length of time while others were allowed to dismiss.

It was obvious that something was afoot and on returning to the hut we were to find that all the palliasses had been removed and that we were to be deprived of these major comforts until further notice.

After the initial shock, steps were taken to alleviate the position by transferring all the bed boards from the bottom bunk to the top bunk thus forming at least a solid base on which to sleep, while the occupant of the bottom bunk slept on the floor beneath. This arrangement, although extremely uncomfortable was to last for a week with no sign of the restoration of the palliasses.

Many wild schemes were broached, even to the extent of storming the main stores under force of numbers and retrieving what we considered our property. After many hut conferences a plan was devised and John the hut leader was detailed to acquaint all the huts in the vicinity to standby at short notice to assist in every way possible by engaging the attentions of the few Jerries left on duty during the changing of the guard.

This occurred regularly at dusk a few minutes before 'lock-up' when all the lights came on, and called for very accurate timing and a close watch on the time of departure of the outgoing guard. Diversions were to be arranged to coincide with the main onslaught on the stores shed in the front compound, while careful examination of the locks and bars on the great doors during daylight hours convinced us that the operation was possible, if the timing was exactly right. It was a question of surprise, but the surprise factor would be short lived and could last no more than five minutes before the new guard arrived.

The time of assault was chosen, runners were sent in all directions to warn the others involved in this combined operation, while the members of our hut strolled nonchalantly through the double gates into the front compound to be in position as dusk fell, each to retrieve one palliasse apiece.

As the outgoing guard retired, a motley collection of forbidden tools was silently brought into use and with some difficulty the doors were forced back revealing a pitch black interior. No allowance had been made for this alarming discovery and several minutes were lost in discovering the exact position of our quarry stacked high to the roof in one corner of the huge building.

Time was pressing and in the general confusion and total darkness progress was painfully slow in selecting a cumbersome palliasse and making for the door in the company of several others, who inevitably tripped over the step to land in a howling heap from which all thoughts of urgency had departed. Our well laid plans had become a shambles. We were soon to discover that it was impossible to run with these large straw filled slippery burdens and yet keep a line of sight on the main gates of our compound still some thirty yards away. One fell, then others followed, unable to alter course in their headlong flight and the narrow confines of the main gate soon became jammed with fallen men tripped by their precious cargoes. Those involved collapsed into howls of laughter incapable of further movement as the throng pressed forward upon them until the heap was six feet deep in men and palliasses and the gate impassable.

The Jerries arrived at the run anxious to check on the cause of the hilarity, and as the lights went on their faces became wreathed in smiles of relief and pleasure as they viewed the evident discomfort of those unable to extricate themselves from the bottom of the pile. One might say that the exercise was a failure, but within two days we were officially allowed to collect our palliasses, and this we did in an orderly fashion. News of the episode was received with undisguised pleasure by the other 'Kriegies', and served as a useful practice run for future forays.

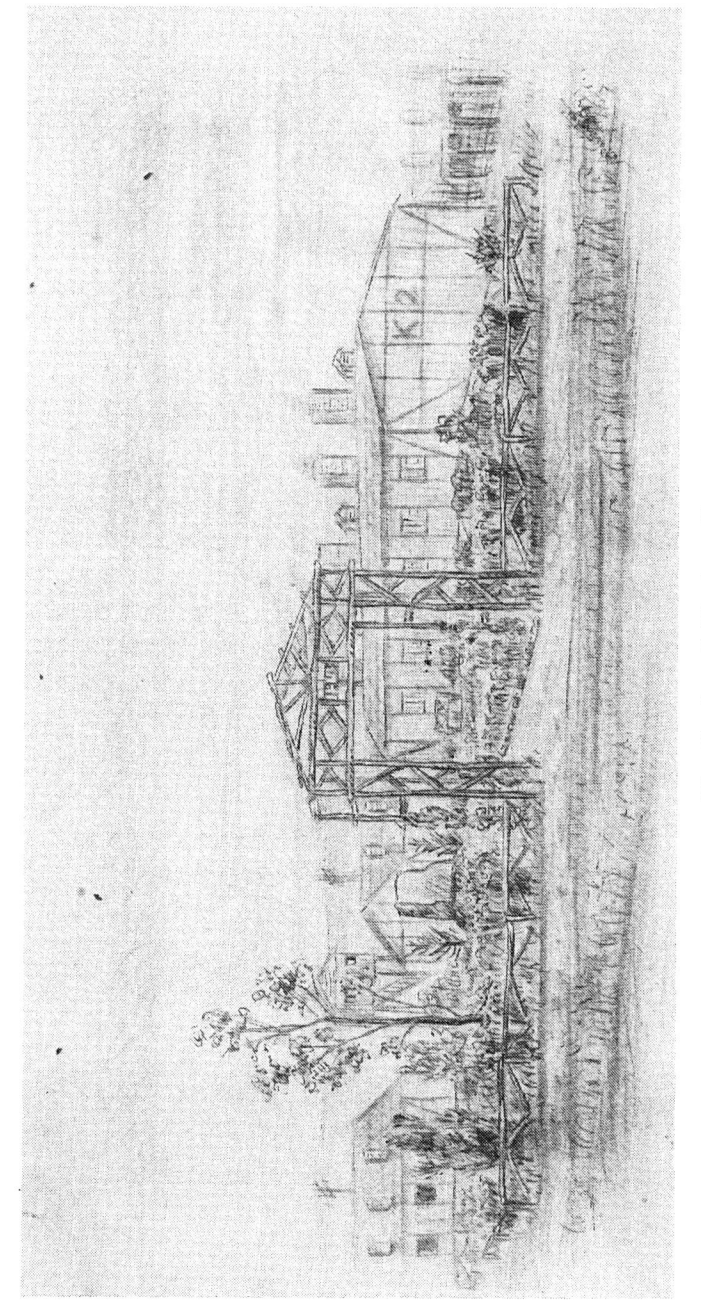

The Garden, Fallingbostell.

*Day and Night
Fallingbostell, Sept. 9th 1944*

STALAG 357
FALLINGBOSTELL
GERMANY

Menu
° ° ° °

FRIED BACON & EGG SANDWICH
TURNIP & SWEDE
BISCUIT BUTTER & MARMALADE
COFFEE

. . .

DEUTSCH SOUP
CHRISTMAS PUDDING
CREAM
TEA

. . .

TOASTED KAM SANDWICH
CHRISTMAS CAKE
TOAST BUTTER & JAM
TEA

. . .

CORNED BEEF & POTATO PIE
CHRISTMAS PUDDING & CREAMED RICE
CREAM
COFFEE

Michael Wilworth
Michael Wiggins
Bruce ____

Christmas Menu, Fallingbostell.

Two of the signatures above are of fellow escapees.

Dear Mother & Dad, This is written in almost total darkness: at one time we could afford to burn our meagre ration of margarine in home-made lamps, but now it's too valuable — too necessary. Every few weeks we receive just enough Red + parcels for one quarter issue, perhaps a third on rare occasions: and still our numbers mount up, the camp grows daily. If other rations, which at times are considerably cut, cease altogether we shall be in a very precarious position, but I think by that time it will all be over bar the shouting.

I was up fairly early this morning for some unknown reason, and as I drank a cup of ersatz coffee, the thought flashed sharply across my mind, 'Oh! to go downstairs to breakfast now, in front of a crackling fire — mother hovering around.'

I don't know why, but I still hope to be home within my year. Could be: great things have happened and great things will happen, they'll have to! Rebel is very cheesed: he feels the cold very much. When light allows, I write; otherwise I sleep. Have not had any letters for weeks. Hope everyone is well yet. Hoping always to hear from you. Yours Benny

Letter home - never posted due to camp conditions

Beyond the Wire

Typhoon Attack

Relief of the Camp, April 1945

Graves of the Crew - Maastricht Cemetery

Chapter 8

Rumours spread that a Red Cross parcel delivery had been seen to arrive in the camp, and hut leaders were dispatched to check that each hut received its share of whatever was issued. In better times it had been one parcel per man but now that the R.A.F. had bombed almost every railway junction within range, the deliveries were infrequent.

Each hut was to receive a limited number of parcels and to be scrupulously fair these were divided up by drawing lots on unspecified items so that everyone had something which they could later swap if they so desired.

Many 'Kriegies' managed their affairs based on the groups or 'combines' originally arranged at the daily bread-cutting ritual, the groups retaining their own joint store cupboard and living as a unit. By this pooling of resources a highly nutritious mash of rice and sultanas or currants could be stewed up on the infernal 'Klim' machine and enjoyed by all, the added flavour of the ensuing smoke screen only enhancing the flavour and the delights to come. Others carefully hoarded all their fruit, which might include prunes and apricots to make a massive brew which was warmed and pressed and left to stand for weeks. The natural yeasts present in the mixture soon resulted in a foaming mass which augured well for the future and at regular intervals samples were taken to see how the brew was progressing. Great interest was shown by the inmates of other huts who also had a brew going and by all those who appeared to be an authority on the subject, of which there were many.

After several weeks of fermentation an old vest was pressed into use to sieve out all the foreign bodies until the remaining liquid was deemed to be clear, though of a very good colour, probably due to the presence of the prunes.

As the official day of 'tasting' arrived, members of other huts were allowed a spoonful of the beverage to vote on flavour and alcohol content, and so judge between the brews. This was considered a ceremony of some importance and only the 'Kriegies' of some years standing with brewing experience over the years of captivity were actually allowed to cast a vote. Now it only required a birthday or similar anniversary to occur among the members of the brewing syndicate to form an excuse for a mass attack upon the brew, which upon empty stomachs soon had a large number of inmates reeling.

Evening roll call under these conditions took even longer than usual as those affected fell out of their huts to be man-handled into line, while friends who were still capable attempted to support them in an upright position while being counted. It was a scene broken by helpless laughter when the confused Jerries repeatedly miscounted as heads bobbed up and fell away to reappear elsewhere, and after three attempts they were forced to give up the unequal struggle and report all correct.

Such were the time consuming small delights of P.O.W. life, and when the chance of a 'wooding-party' came up each hut jumped at the chance of temporary freedom outside the wire.

The huge wagons, normally drawn by four horses, with a central shaft, were ideal for the purpose and with upwards of a hundred 'Kriegies' pulling and pushing from behind, we made good progress out of the main gate towards the surrounding forest. Though accompanied by armed guards with their fearsome companions, it was with a feeling of suppressed excitement that we entered the depths of the forest and savoured the damp musty smells and the soft ground underfoot.

Thoughts of rapid escape immediately filled the mind, but common sense prevailed with the realisation that the chances were nil and that every well trained dog was just waiting for the exercise. We would not make the first hundred yards, apart from the risk of the odd bullet. On reaching the working area, the Jerries formed a wide ring around us and we were left to our own devices. Saws and axes were provided and we all thoroughly enjoyed the experience though quickly realising that due to falling rations our original strength and stamina had deserted us and we were soon exhausted.

Returning to camp with the fully loaded wagon was as much as we could manage and the remainder of the day was spent resting. On this pretext we retained one saw and one axe to chop up the load next morning, after which we were somehow able to conceal these most valuable tools for our own personal use, though naturally not in our own hut, which was inevitably thoroughly searched.

As the chill of autumn set in, those huts that had built up a supply of wood began to light the big black stoves at each end of the hut, both for warmth at night and to dry their washing which hung suspended in tattered shrouds, a large part of which had seen better days. Despite the conditions and the shortage of food most 'Kriegies' kept remarkably healthy and serious disease was almost unknown, though many long serving members were said to 'have gone round the bend' after years of soul destroying captivity, and had become very eccentric in their dress and manners.

The oldest inhabitant, or rather the longest time served member, was said to have been shot down in an Anson over the channel on the second day of the war, but as he had become rather withdrawn and aloof no one had been able to verify the fascinating details of his brave entry into the war and his even more rapid exit. He was one of the 'best blue brigade'. One such member resided in our hut on a top bunk near the door, and he was always, on principle, the last to leave his bed at morning roll call, and would only do so after a pistol was thrust in his ear. It was almost a daily ritual and we would hang back to witness this awe-inspiring sight wondering who would crack first, the silent 'Kriegie', or the apoplectic Jerry. The 'Kriegie' always won but we picked up some fine Germanic swear words. He would finally condescend to drop to the floor and join us on parade, having once more driven the Jerry to despair.

Life in the camp oscillated between the dull and the hilarious, and when a new influx of R.A.F. arrived there was a concerted rush to the wire of the inner compound to check the faces of the newcomers, and to hear at first hand of their latest exploits. We were still receiving regular wireless reports of the course of the war, but it was nothing like hearing the facts from someone who had just come from home, and had all the latest gen on the V1 and V2 attacks on London.

This latter interest had been aroused because we had been hearing strange unusual sounds morning and evening when the wind had been in the North, denoting some unknown activity emanating from the coast of Germany. These noises consisted of a dull roar coupled with a rushing sound which went on for some seconds and we had convinced ourselves that they were V2 rockets on the way to England. No one was able to verify these theories, and even the Jerries we spoke to had no knowledge of the phenomenon.

The new inmates soon settled into the camp routine but were somewhat depressed at the size of the daily rations and began to haunt the rear of the Jerry cook-house for the odd swede or turnip like everyone else.

Other huts took their turn to go out on wooding-parties while most of us attended one of the rare funerals which took place in the camp. Our hut was not involved, but everyone went on parade, including senior German officers, but it was an R.A.F. parade, vastly different from the usual scrappy turn-out we offered the Jerries, to stand for the service taken by our own padre. We were then brought to attention as the Last Post was sounded for one who after all his earlier terrors and later trials was not to return home, but be buried in a foreign land. It was a most moving and solemn occasion as the simple coffin draped in the Union Jack wound its way out of the compound preceded by a lone piper and attended by the R.A.F. senior officers and friends. The sad lament of the piper could still be heard as the little cortège disappeared on its way to the small cemetery in the depths of the forest outside the wire.

As the dark evenings drew in, those 'combines' that had precious tea reserved for such occasions, would brew up and we would sit and talk for hours of the future and what we might be doing in a year's time. We were now quite certain that the war was going in our favour and that it was only a question of time before we would be free to restart our lives.

Many of us had never had a proper job, knowing that war was coming and some had only just left school before joining up, thus having little knowledge of civilian life, having spent four or five years in the R.A.F.

It was remarkable how many favoured a return to the soil, to be farmers, small holders, but above all to be self-employed, and to be in control of their own destiny, perhaps a reflection of their original wish to volunteer for air-crew duties. We were simply an individually minded collection of people averse to bull for its own sake, and in many ways camp life, though confined, was not unbearable, but the sense of boredom was considerable.

The possibility of near starvation was becoming a major topic of conversation, to such an extent that 'Kriegies' would often erupt into flights of fancy as to what they would dream up for their next meal, listing all their favourite foods.

Comfort was not particularly high on the agenda as the exigencies of service life had accustomed us to make the best of things, but warmth was paramount, and to a limited extent this was within our grasp.

When the shout came that an empty baker's cart had been seen behind the cook-house, our hut swung into action. The two huge stoves had all but consumed our winnings from the wooding-party, and our spies were always on the look-out for further supplies, as were the members of other huts. But we had first spied the cart and realised its potential, thus making a claim and acquainting adjacent huts, so that they were aware of our intentions and would cooperate in the usual manner.

In the late afternoon, Rebel and I amongst others were set to keep an eye on the cart and assess which tools might be required for rapid dismantling by strolling nonchalantly past the object of our intentions, while keeping a sharp look out for the possible return of the horse which would perforce put an end to all operations. Bringing into use all our previous experience of rapid deployment, the attempt was made at dusk, with the assistance of other 'Kriegies' creating minor noisy disturbances near the scene of operations, thus covering the sounds of our frenzied attack.

The scheme worked to perfection, with runners dispatched to carry larger sections of the cart back to the hut where other teams with saw and axe took turns in converting the remains into small manageable pieces which were immediately hidden in false ceilings and behind cupboards. As the lights came on, the scene was deserted, all the signs of the struggle had been erased and we were all gently strolling back to our huts to await lock-up.

Next morning early, those involved waited eagerly for the return of the horse and driver, and from a safe distance witnessed the strange antics of the Jerry as he turned the corner of the cook-house in readiness to harness up his cart. Only two wheels and the harness remained to meet his startled gaze.

Reprisals were soon to come. Next morning, every hut in close proximity was locked and barred while the inmates were on 'appel'; and for the remainder of the day we wandered the compounds cadging drinks and scraps of food in exchange for a first hand account of our recent exploits. Earlier reports on the 'grape-vine' had preceded us and the full details were relished by those further afield. We did not go hungry that day, the lock-out had in no way discomforted us, and we had put one over on the Jerries by greatly increasing our supply of firewood at little cost to ourselves.

Chapter 9

A great deal of planning went into these minor operations and when the hut next door asked us for assistance in what appeared to be a similar harebrained scheme we were only too willing to help. Our view was that as the Jerries were no longer adhering to the Geneva Convention in keeping us supplied with food and warmth in acceptable quantities, we were quite within our rights to take things into our own hands wherever and whenever possible. This latest plan proposed the major removal of part of the ablutions, which took the form of long wooden troughs a foot deep and perhaps four feet wide with two rows of taps overhead to serve both sides. The huge affair was roofed in but open to one end and this simple fact made the whole idea possible. Detailed inspections were carried out and as so much wood was involved, two huts agreed to share the proceeds and were thus involved in the joint conference to discover just what was required in the way of tools. Most of these were communal property, but their exact whereabouts were often uncertain at any given time. It had been decided that as the long troughs had been built and fitted in units approximately twenty feet long it was the end unit of the system that was the obvious choice for removal. There was an inordinate amount of washing done that day as a succession of operators using hard won screwdrivers and knives of all sorts attempted to unscrew the fastenings holding the water pipes to the long overhead beam which was part of the structure to be removed. Look-outs were posted to check for approaching goons as the screws were removed with difficulty and pushed back in by hand to support the long lengths of pipes pending the final concerted rush.

As dusk fell the two huts involved sent out their strongest members to wash yet again, and with fifteen aside these stalwarts uplifted the unit and at the run very soon delivered it to a hut where it was skilfully twisted to pass through the door into willing hands. It was immediately cut in half so that the hut next door had their share, and both huts, in a carefully planned exercise involving all the occupants on saw and axe very soon reduced the ungainly mass into a heap of cherished firewood in lengths suitable for concealment.

The final operation had taken less than twenty minutes and was considered a great success, particularly as the ablutions remaining were more than adequate. Naturally the Jerries took a dim view and we were subjected to the interminable Germanic 'ear-bashing' on 'appel' the next morning. Though not entirely understanding every word, it transpired that we were to be without lights for a week, a small price to pay.

Most of us listened with mock attention to these frequent diatribes, without exception fascinated by the strong guttural tones raised to fever pitch by anger and complaint, convinced that the German language was far superior to any other for this purpose. Now that we were to be without lights for a week, steps were immediately put in hand to render down part of our hard won store of margarine specifically put aside for this eventuality. It was a slow and careful process, but the resultant oil was found to be clear and slow burning using a small wick at one end of a specially constructed container, on the principle of the old Roman lamps. We were not to be beaten and invariably found the antidote to any hardship thrust upon us, apart from the question of rations which was beyond our control.

This was a matter of increasing anxiety as the year wore on and the underlying seriousness of the position was brought home to us most forcibly one morning while doing our usual circuit of the compound. A group of 'Kriegies' had assembled round the huge septic tank at the outfall of the latrines. There was no laughter or the usual chat associated with such gatherings but rather a deadly determined hush and those nearby rushed over thinking that some one had fallen in.

But this was no accident; the reverse was the case. The members of the hut concerned were carrying out their own form of summary justice to one who had been convicted of concealing a slice of bread, the property of another. In normal times this might be considered of no consequence, but in the present climate it reflected the depth of feeling occasioned by this despicable act, and the thief was now immersed in the effluent. We watched in silent horror as the culprit surfaced to be repeatedly submerged by outraged fellows, until one by one they drifted away satisfied that the required punishment had been meted out. No words were said, the whole affair had been carried out in silence, thus adding to the tense atmosphere as the miscreant clambered out on to dry land and proceeded to walk the circuit in an attempt to dry off, an outcast. It was not an edifying sight but a lesson to all as to how human nature could react in exceptional circumstances.

The general consensus was that the punishment fitted the crime though the majority quietly hoped that the episode would not be repeated.

At the approach of the festive season 'Kriegies' were concerned about getting a letter home in time for Christmas, and with this in mind began to decorate the limited space available on the edge of the letters in appropriate fashion. The issue of letters and cards was strictly rationed and liable to censorship but we hoped that the Jerries would allow our artistic attempts to pass through unchecked.

Despite the depressing state of the daily rations situation, everyone was determined to try and celebrate Christmas in the usual manner and for weeks choice items of previous Red Cross parcels had been religiously put aside to make the occasion something to be remembered. Meanwhile hunger pangs were forgotten in a concerted build-up for the magnificent spread to come.

'Combines' vied with each other in revealing rare commodities long hidden in secret places. Small tins of ham, corned beef, creamed rice and even Christmas cake and pudding came to light to be dusted off and polished in readiness. Pots of jam and marmalade appeared as if by magic, silent proof of the sustained will power of the 'Kriegies' who had denied themselves these pleasures over a long period, for just such an occasion.

Menus were drawn up in detail giving tantalising glimpses of the delights to come, including the added bonus of real coffee rather than the ersatz offered by the Jerries. All this self-denial had been made possible by supplementing the daily rations with whatever was to be found at the rear of the Jerry cook-house, sometimes just peelings, at other times whole potatoes or swedes, which were now considered a delicacy, raw or cooked. The only other source of items were the Jerry guards who could never refuse a packet of cigarettes for a loaf of bread or occasionally a lump of coarse bacon, but cigarettes were now becoming increasingly valuable and non-smokers were welcome members of the poverty-stricken 'combines' now that they had become the bankers of the community. Certain huts, well respected for the excellence of their brew had taken on the joint responsibility of starting a Christmas special.

Some weeks earlier, runners had gone round the compound with the shout "Special brew starting in hut 49. All types of fruit welcome - report to hut 49!" and this had brought a good response. Anyone offering the basic material became automatic shareholders, in the distribution of the final essence, and many 'combines' had joined forces to secure this additional timely uplift.

Stoves not normally lit until evening were well away early in the morning to herald Christmas Day and an unhealthy pall of smoke hung over the compound in the still air. At roll-call, inmates rushed out of their huts to behave impeccably on parade, not wishing to antagonise the Jerries and therefore delay the proceedings, as was their usual habit.

Back in the huts, the long forgotten aromas of cooked breakfasts once again filled the air as each 'combine' tended their precious items sizzling away in home made pots and pans on the tops of the stoves. Carefully hoarded cigarettes and tobacco were handed round, a fitting complement to the delights of real coffee with a touch of 'Klim' powdered milk, a rare commodity. Later, the camp church resounded with the well loved seasonal hymns, and all present entered into the spirit of the occasion, surrounded by their fellows, yet captive in a foreign land.

The remainder of the day passed in happy anticipation as duty cooks toiled at the stoves to set even more delectable offerings before their 'combines' already seated expectantly at the rickety tables. With hollow stomachs at last full, the evening ended in hazy contentment as the special brew was passed round in final celebration of a long remembered day. To add to our satisfaction, the latest news on the progress of the invading armies had been the talk of the Christmas period and the wireless operators had been listening out on all possible occasions at great personal risk. The general feeling was that they merited a 'gong' for their untiring efforts in going beyond the call of duty in their specialised subject, and deserved some form of recognition. The news that airborne troops and gliders had again been in operation brought me to the realisation that my brother Dick would be involved now that the demands on Ferry Command had become less. Huge numbers of R.A.F. men would have no doubt been drawn in from other branches to assist in this major effort, particularly as the flow of new aircraft from America was not so urgent now that we had such an efficient home production.

I could imagine that my brother was now taking an active part in the shooting war, and fell to wondering if he had been engaged in the 'drop' on the Low countries, where a veritable armada of tug aircraft and gliders must have filled the skies over England before crossing the channel on the way to the drop zones. We felt somehow cheated not to have seen it and not to have been in at the end, particularly as that work-horse of the R.A.F., the Halifax, would no doubt be leading the way.

We stood isolated in a separate world, no longer in touch with the realities of war, unaware of the precise details of the day to day position of the Allies and more importantly the successes and setbacks of our own forces as bridgeheads were held and lost and won again. We had only the news the B.B.C. was permitted to broadcast and were no longer the recipients of classified information which we had once been. But it was the news and the hopes for the future that kept us going through the grim winter months with little other comfort to sustain us.

The days dragged and the nights were worse, as we could no longer afford to keep the stoves going for long periods and it was so cold that we longed for the daylight when we could at least keep warm by walking the circuit.

A fall of snow brought a little light relief and another element into our lives, as snowball fights became the main form of exercise and sundry 'goons' received the odd misdirected missile in good humour.

The daily rations, on which we now totally relied, remained at a slice of coarse rye bread and two bowls of soup, or an occasional mash of sauerkraut which we had unwillingly begun to relish. It was quite amazing how one actually looked forward to the twice daily delivery of soup, which could only be classed as 'slops'. We only hoped that German P.O.W.s fared better and would have been ashamed if they had not. The acorn coffee we were offered, we had to admit was a clever substitute, but bore no resemblance to the real thing, being just a pale brown liquid with an earthy flavour, but welcomed nevertheless.

As the cold held us in an icy grip we were again running out of firewood and were reduced to burning some of our precious bed boards to raise the temperature of the hut a trifle for short periods, generally before going to bed. This only added to the discomfort as palliasses ballooned out between the remaining boards and the straw inside became gradually reduced to chaff with its inherent dust to fall upon the occupant below.

And then suddenly our prayers were answered. A stack of huge wooden poles arrived in the compounds, waiting, we presumed, to be erected along the outer perimeter wire to increase the lighting. Similar to telephone posts, they were about forty feet long and a foot across at the butt, each one the equivalent of enough firewood to see us through the worst of the winter. The ablution troughs had already been further decimated in the interim, with consequent reprisals and this latest windfall was to be a life-saver.

Though it was every man for himself, a conference was called in order to gain maximum benefit from this unexpected offering, without the Jerries noticing the gradual depletion of their stock. It was assumed that the Jerries who had actually delivered the poles would probably have no connection with those detailed to carry out the final erection and therefore several of the poles could safely be removed with impunity and without arousing suspicion. Several huts benefited immediately without discovery and after a suitable interval, other huts claimed possession until the stack became seriously depleted and only half a dozen poles remained.

The procedure was simple though demanding a great deal of effort on our part, as the solid timber was a dead weight and many men were required to lift and run with these long cumbersome slippery burdens at the risk at least of a broken ankle in the event of an unfortunate accident. Only the strongest fittest members of a hut were considered for this operation while the remainder waited in the hut, saw and axe at the ready. These took turns in a fury of destruction until the recognisable pole was rendered harmless and safely stowed away in rapid time.

These events all took place at dusk with look-outs posted, but lack of planning on the part of one hut led to all the inmates being caught in the act, an embarrassing situation for which there was no ready answer.

On every recent morning 'appel' we had been half expecting the reprisals denoting the discovery of our misdeeds and at last it had come. The hut convicted was to be without lights and palliasses for a week while the whole compound was reduced to walking the circuit for the remainder of the day, all huts being locked and barred.

It had been a long parade, but highly amusing as the senior R.A.F. officer attempted to translate in measured tones, the ravings and gesticulations of a highly excited camp commandant.

During the lock-out our huts had been meticulously searched and various 'verboten' tools brought to light and confiscated thus limiting any further large scale forays. The remaining poles were subsequently removed and erected at the end of the compound where a large assembly of 'Kriegies' overlooked the work and attempted to assist the operation as much as possible by getting in the way and offering such encouraging remarks as "Deutchland *unter* Alles", and "Hitler ist kaput", which brought answering cheers from the onlookers. We were by this time becoming very uppish and independent and could almost sense the light at the end of the tunnel. The enemy was now being pressed on all sides and at last we, as a nation, had the upper hand, though few of the Jerries we spoke to had much knowledge of the course of the war.

We supposed that eventually our advancing troops would over-run the camp and we would be released at the end of the war which must result in our victory. It was significant that in the whole of our P.O.W. life, no-one doubted the final outcome. Meanwhile we endured the long cold winter, somewhat mitigated by the now roaring stoves lit only in the late afternoon to conserve fuel. Outside, the early March winds seared the compound as we continued our regular perambulations of the circuit to exercise our thinning frames, despite the razor-sharp blast.

It was good to return to the warmth of the huts after evening roll-call and brew up a mug of tea which was to get weaker and thinner following repeated attempts at extracting the maximum value from a given quantity of tea. Nothing was wasted; even the swede and turnip peelings thrown out from the Jerry cook-house were seized upon to reinforce the daily soup rations. There were now virtually no reserves left from previous Red Cross parcels and we came to rely more and more on what could be bartered from the Jerry guards in exchange for what few cigarettes remained in circulation.

It was a grim period sustained only by the daily wireless reports of impressive gains despite set backs at the Dutch rivers, where the enemy had been making use of these natural lines of defence.

The British 2nd Army had taken Antwerp and Maastricht, and Montgomery was advancing along the Rhine. It was great news and kept us in our huts until the news-reader had made his daily rounds, while the compound was deserted, everyone determined not to miss the latest gen even if there were 'goons' about. And then came the reports of another huge airborne drop beyond the Rhine, of gliders carrying troops, some with artillery and light tanks, and we were convinced that only the Halifax would be capable of getting this armada airborne.

There was uproar when we learned that the Rhine had been crossed and was now in our hands. Shouts echoed across the compound, "They're only 200 miles away!" and from the more cautious residents, "Home in times for Christmas!" The atmosphere was electric, but soon to be quenched.

The Jerries were rattled and we were to be moved again. But where? There was nowhere else to go now that General Zhukov and the Russians had entered Germany from the East, and the American 3rd Army was approaching from the South.

The rumour had persisted for some days and there was a lot of 'duff gen' about as the German Authorities were always very secretive about their plans and no definite orders had materialised. Some claimed, speculating on the tortuous machinations of the German mentality, that on the last day of the war there would still be found 'Kriegies' being marched backwards and forwards between the advancing armies.

The thought of marching East away from our own advancing troops and in fact towards the Russkies brought consternation. To avert this dire possibility various wild escape ideas were discussed and plans were laid to make use of any opportunity that might arise, but as to when and where, that would depend on conditions at the time. And then a small wagon of Red Cross parcels arrived in the camp and that decided us. Food was an essential item for an escape attempt to have the slightest chance of success and small groups of 'Kriegies' with faint confidence, aware of the efficiency of the enemy, hatched various schemes to cover any eventuality.

It was obviously impossible to plan a mass escape which would bring dire and immediate retribution, but it was thought that small numbers might make it, given the opportunity, particularly if it was to be a march and not a rail movement.

After several anxious days while rumours and counter rumours sped about the camp, our final marching orders were announced. We were to fall in and march to another camp, in which direction or how far we knew not, but it was evident that the exodus would take some days as provision had been made for night-stops at prearranged sites where we would be fed and allowed to rest.

This information clinched the idea and Mike, Buzz and I, having already been offered a quantity of porridge oats and other useful gut-fillers by those who wished us well, were now determined to succeed.

On the morning of departure, with bags slung over shoulders containing our few treasured possessions we were all on parade awaiting final orders. At the last minute there had been an issue of a loaf apiece of bread to last the journey and this was a luxury that was to make everything possible.

Four abreast, in a long winding untidy column we left the now deserted camp, with the guards spaced at twenty foot intervals on both sides with alert dogs at heel. It did not auger well. The sparse heathland offered no cover as far as one could see and only groups of graceful silver birch broke the horizon. And we were marching East. Every two or three hours we were halted and allowed to drop where we stood on the rough track to rest for a few minutes, while those wanting to relieve themselves were allowed to the edge of the track.

As the day wore on we began to realise how unfit we were, and that near starvation rations had taken their toll of our stamina. Doubts arose of our capability to make the final dash, but when low scrub and pine trees began to reach towards the edges of the track, hope returned and with it, strength.

The three of us had not spoken much during the march, acutely aware of the proximity of the guards, and the noise of their jangling accoutrements rang in our ears. We now began to assess our chances in the light of the setting sun and the increase in the roadside vegetation. Mike suddenly said, "I think we ought to go now, the Jerries may call a halt at any time and then we've had it!"

Buzz did not immediately answer but I said, "I think it is too soon - too light, we'd never make it." As if to prove the point, there was a sudden commotion up ahead, dogs barked and a volley of shots rang out. We never knew the outcome, whether they made it to freedom, or ran back into the shelter of their marching comrades who would quickly embrace them back into the fold. And so we waited, containing our impatience to be gone. As dusk began to fall it was now or never, and with whispered warnings to those around us we waited momentarily until low scrub surrounded us. We slowly worked our way to the right of the column to a position immediately behind a Jerry guard while others fell in close astern masking the view of those behind, and like three owls drifted silently into the forest. The half expected shots and shouts did not come; we turned and ran, exulting in our new found freedom. We ran on for what seemed miles before tripping over unseen roots in the near total darkness of the forest to collapse in an exhausted heap, speechless and gasping for breath. We felt we could go no further.

It took a long time to recover our strength but we all agreed that we should put as much distance as possible between ourselves and the column, and struggled on to walk all night in a westerly direction using the North Star as a guide.

When we had been originally shot down we had had special compass buttons sewn onto our battle-dress for just such an emergency, but these had long since disappeared. We had no maps or any other guide, apart from the sun by day and the stars at night.

A certain amount of delayed shock now set in, which, coupled with our complete exhaustion forced us to lay up for most of the next day while making inroads on our food supply to build up lost stamina.

We had at first decided to move only by night and hide up during the day to escape detection, which seemed the natural thing to do, but after several scares while travelling at night we were to reverse our decision. In open country, night movements were comparatively simple, one could see odd fences and ditches and streams, but in the depths of the forest areas which we frequently traversed, the complete and utter darkness made progress painfully slow and sometimes noisy, a factor we could not ignore. What was of equal importance was the loss of all sense of direction when the stars were no longer visible. The encounter which occurred on the second night brought us swiftly to our senses.

We were traversing the edge of a small copse, travelling quietly which we had now trained ourselves to do when suddenly a match flared not twenty feet away. In the few seconds it took to light two cigarettes our surroundings came to life. There were German tanks on all sides, the black crosses stark and fearsome in the flickering light and all the paraphernalia of war was imprinted on the mind in that split second.

In line astern, we froze. With a hand out-thrust, I motioned a silent reversal and in a manfully controlled retreat we departed in shocked silence. It was ages before we could bring ourselves to speak, our minds fully occupied in putting as much distance as possible from the hair-raising scene.

If this was travelling at night it took all the icing off the gingerbread and we did not need any more shocks, as we were already living on our nerves.

Later, resting after our exertions Buzz asked, "What are tanks doing so far back from the front?" and Mike chipped in, "Perhaps they're dug in, short of fuel. Do you remember we heard on the news that the Jerries were now short of fuel as a result of all the bombing?"

"Very likely," I added, "but how on earth the Jerries did not see or hear our approach until we were well into their encampment, we shall never know!"

"I'll tell you what," said Mike, "if that Jerry had not lit a fag at that precise moment we would have tripped over a bloody great pile of ammo, and we would have been back inside or worse."

It was a sobering thought and from that moment we decided to move by day. We could at least see the enemy and take cover when necessary.

It was impossible to gauge the distance travelled each day, but we were not concerned as each day would bring us nearer to the front-line, though we lost count of the actual days. We were now making good progress in daylight and the countryside was changing from heathland to part plough-land where the going was difficult.

For days we had been walking over the equivalent of Salisbury Plain and tank tracks stretched to the horizon criss-crossing the vast plain as far as one could see, though happily no tanks appeared, for which we were grateful as cover was non-existent.

Then we had to traverse acres of swamp land where to miss one's footing from the great humps and tussocks meant losing a boot in the mire beneath and we hoped no-one was watching us, as it would have been impossible to hastily extricate ourselves from the treacherous terrain.

Chapter 10

So far in daylight we had not seen a soul in this vast uninhabited landscape, not a farm, or signs of cattle or people, though huge wooden barns littered the open spaces. But this was to change.

One evening just before dusk as we were considering stopping for the night we saw in the distance a small shepherd's hut and decided to investigate, because this would be the ideal place for a brew-up and an opportunity to make a dish of our long awaited porridge. We had tried chewing it dry, but it stuck in the throat, and we were now eagerly looking forward to this luxury, a small amount of milk powder having been reserved for the purpose.

Approaching the hut silently and with great caution on the windowless side, the thought having already occurred to us that there might be an occupant, we crept up close to the wall and listened, our hearts hammering and almost holding our breath before peering in at the window. It was empty, and evidently not in regular use, though the rough fireplace in the corner showed signs of recent occupation.

After a brief conference the decision was made. We had seen no-one all day and there were no cattle or sheep in sight and this was the ideal hide-out in which to spend the night. Gathering twigs and leaves Mike soon had a small fire going and keeping the rising smoke to a minimum we enjoyed our first cup of tea since leaving camp. It was all very civilised, and leaning back on boxes and broken stools we celebrated the occasion with a rare cigarette and congratulated ourselves on our progress.

We had all we wanted, or almost all. Water had been no problem, as we always topped up our water containers from the many streams and ditches we crossed and we carried our own home-made cooking utensils.

Getting down to the serious business of making the porridge, Mike measured out what he thought we should need and stirred the whole lot together while I cut the bread. Buzz was involved in carrying out a minute inspection of the hut and as Mike went on gently stirring the porridge another sound began slowly to insinuate itself.

Alarm bells rang. Buzz raised a finger from his vantage point near the window. Had the smoke been seen? From days of living rough our ears were attuned to every sound, and now there was no disguising the metallic clink of a fully armed German soldier on the move. Buzz went quickly to the window and whispered, "One Jerry soldier - no more in sight! We'll have to brazen it out. Be as normal as possible!"

There was a hasty discussion. We would be foreign labour working on the farm with little knowledge of the language. Our variety of great coats might assist in this deception. Buzz would engage the enemy in broken German to try to allay any suspicion of our true identity. After all, the Jerry would hardly expect British P.O.W.s to be making porridge in a shepherd's hut in the middle of nowhere.

We were to be found assiduously attending to the porridge when the German flung back the door of the hut with the expected tirade.

Germans always seemed angry, but perhaps it was just the language. "Was ist - was ist los?" to which Buzz replied as best he knew, that we were having our supper. "Ist nicht gut!" went on the German, uncertain of his ground, and then in a rising voice, "Kommen sie hier!" This was a phrase we well knew - Come with me - and at this point things looked a bit grim, but after a short interval Buzz was able to return to the fray with the immortal words, "Wir sind Dutch arbeiter," and continued at some length in his fractured German.

At this the soldier relaxed somewhat but was obviously far from satisfied and after looking keenly at us, stomped off into the gathering twilight. "Well done, mate! What did you say to him?" asked Mike, after a stunned silence which we hesitated to break, not believing our luck.

"I simply said that we were having our supper," replied Buzz. "That we were Dutch labourers from the local farm."

"When the Jerry shouted 'Come with me,' I thought we'd had it," I replied. "How did you get away with it?"

"I think I said that we'd finished work," replied Buzz, "and that after our supper, we would return to the farm for the night."

"I hope he won't come back with a platoon of Jerries!" remarked Mike, and this thought was uppermost in our minds as we returned to our interrupted meal.

Fortunately the fire had by now gone out under the porridge which was not burnt but still warm, and our recent experience was not allowed to spoil the occasion.

We were however on tenderhooks, continually wondering what one German soldier was doing in this wilderness. One soldier meant that there must be others and could they possibly have heard of the escape, now some thirty miles behind us?

Our knowledge of the German doggedness and efficiency told us that this was a distinct possibility, and that they might even now be watching the hut from a distance. Voicing these thoughts, Mike suddenly announced, "I'm not going to be able to sleep here tonight, and if we can't sleep we can't keep alert!"

In a sudden flurry of agreement we hastily gathered all our gear together and stole out into the night. A pressing urgency consumed us. It was now almost dark though no stars were yet visible as we proceeded on our original course to put as many miles as possible between ourselves and the recent confrontation. Walking quickly and silently, and stopping every few minutes to listen, straining eyes and ears for any unusual night sounds we finally took cover in a small spinney confident at last of comparative safety. Wrapping ourselves in our great coats, we slept soundly.

The cawing of rooks and the chatter of jays woke us to a misty dawn, and these were welcome sounds as proof that we were alone. Making a hearty breakfast of dry bread and prunes, we waited for the sun to guide us on our way.

The expected sun did not appear, and remembering what we had learnt about moss growing on trees and how plants reached for the light we were able to orientate ourselves in the right direction.

Filling our water containers from a nearby stream and crossing the plank bridge we walked along under the cover of the tall reeds bordering the stream. Unwilling now to put ourselves at risk by traversing large open spaces, wherever possible we kept to the edges of woods and along hedgelines. The type of country had changed considerably and there were now many more signs of man's recent handiwork, though strangely enough, few signs of human habitation.

We had left behind the comparative desert and marshland of the heath and were now in rolling country where huge fields of lupins stretched almost to the horizon interspersed with newly cultivated ground awaiting other crops.

Great blocks of forest timber stood out dark and menacing on all sides, but we could no longer bring ourselves to walk through them as little light penetrated their wind blown heads and we found the stygian darkness depressing, and the noise of breaking twigs disturbing. But on a dull day the varying shapes of these living monoliths served a useful purpose in being recognisable over long distances and therefore serving as useful bearing points to keep us on track.

It was while traversing along the edge of one of these huge forests that an unusual humming sound was borne in on the westerly wind. "Sounds like tanks on the move," murmured Mike.

"You've got tanks on the brain, Mike. More likely heavy lorries travelling at speed," replied Buzz. "You can hear the tyre hum above the engines," and as we advanced, dim shapes appeared on the horizon between the trees.

It was obviously a main road crossing from North to South, and as we had seen few roads of any consequence in the whole of our travels this had to be a major artery for all forms of transport. We could now see that the road was built-on a causeway with steep road-side banks up which we gingerly climbed on our bellies under cover of small scrub to size up the position.

It was going to be difficult to cross. The noise was deafening as great tank transporters and ammunition lorries passed within a few feet of our noses, mostly going South. We lay under cover for some time, uncertain whether to make a dash for it or wait until dark when headlights might give us more warning of approaching traffic.

Roadside trees masked a blind bend and this factor was the cause of our indecision but with a muffled call of, "Now - Now," we sped across the wide road to tumble down the opposite bank into obscurity.

A couple of jays screeched off in alarm as we came to rest at the bottom of the bank but no other sound broke the stillness, to our great relief, as our sudden descent had been entirely unplanned and for us, unusually noisy. We had become very aware of the importance of keeping a low profile, and were becoming masters of the silent approach, so that any sudden movement of bird or animal caused us to freeze in our tracks, as when the occasional deer, lying up wind of us would suddenly explode into action to crash off through the undergrowth. Apart from the perpetual alertness and sudden shocks we found ourselves enjoying this enforced ramble through the changing countryside. It was strangely peaceful and with the strengthening sun causing long dormant buds to break into leaf every new day announced the arrival of spring and a renewal of life.

The hedges were aglow with wild plum and cherry and the stately silver birch festooned itself in a golden cascade, while the larches threw off their dead twigs and covered themselves with vivid green shoots.

I was reminded of the long walks Dick and I, as boys, used to take with my father far into the country, to return sometimes by bus, exhausted, but happy, to tea and crumpets! There were no crumpets now. In fact our food reserves were soon to become a matter for concern as most of the Red Cross luxuries had disappeared and our supply of bread was dwindling. And then we came upon a lucky find, a huge clamp of turnips.

So far during our travels we had come across nothing even remotely associated with food, not a cabbage or any green-stuffs of any kind in the acres of fields we had inspected. No standing crops remained and we could only assume that this was largely potato land, cultivated, but as yet unplanted.

Upon seeing this great mound of earth in a far corner of a field we almost broke into a run, but common sense prevailed and we approached with our usual caution following the hedgeline round the field until the clamp was within reach. On close inspection it appeared to have lain untouched since the previous autumn, when it was no doubt set up and with sticks and broken branches close at hand, we were soon able to unearth the contents.

The Germans as expected, had made a thorough job of the clamping process using plenty of straw, the turnips were in good condition and we were soon eating the smaller ones like apples. It was an exciting find and great to be able to get one's teeth into something solid for a change.

Packing our bags with several carefully chosen specimens in reserve we covered all signs of our entry by replacing and smoothing down the earth casing and strewing twigs and leaves over all so as not to advertise our passage, a no doubt totally unnecessary exercise that had now become part of our daily life.

We left the scene encouraged, as we now had a nutritious source of energy, something to fill the gut and refreshing to chew on, and having found one clamp there would no doubt be others as we proceeded on our way.

It still surprised us that with all the evident signs of man's activity, we rarely saw any cattle or human habitation and nothing to mar our progress, except the weather which suddenly changed and closed in.

It rained on and off all day and although eager to press on there was no urgency. We were still free and now felt fairly confident of a happy conclusion to our efforts, being quite prepared during the last few exciting days to lie low and await being overrun by our own troops.

To protect ourselves from the down-pour we had constructed a rough hide from the lower branches of the pine trees and set these at an acute angle to the trunk, thus deflecting most of the rain, though it was a pretty miserable occasion, as we had no way of drying out our clothes except by wearing them.

We fell to trying to calculate how much ground we had covered and to place ourselves on an imaginary map but as we had little knowledge of our precise starting point, this was a comparatively useless exercise. All we could be sure about was the fact that we were travelling roughly westwards and though we had no information of our advancing armies for some ten days we could only hope that things were going well for them and that they had left the Rhine far behind. After all, from our point of view, we had not entered into a forced march, we were not fit enough. There had been days when we had probably made little progress over very difficult terrain and at the most our trip had become no more than a steady but alert walk, circumnavigating all sorts of obstacles and taking advantage of available cover wherever possible. We were still in a foreign country and this fact was uppermost in our minds at all times.

The one bright occasion was the vision of an armada of Fortresses on their way South. The weather had cleared and the first intimation of anything unusual was the sound of distant machine gun fire, which came to us as we were creeping along the southern edge of a large wood. Our field of view being somewhat limited, we hurried to the end of the wood uncertain what to expect, but relieved and excited to find the sky apparently filled with aircraft of all kinds. Although quite high, the Fortresses flew in tight formation escorted by their own fighter screen, but in between flew the enemy, attempting to break up the formation and so escape the withering cross-fire from so many bombers intent on covering each other.

We were glad to see that they were being largely successful, though here and there bits and pieces were seen to fly off the advancing horde which nevertheless pressed on overhead towards their objective.

In our excitement we had left the cover of the wood, but very quickly returned to take shelter as spent bullets and bits of damaged aircraft rained down upon us, pattering on the undergrowth like hail, only far more dangerous. "Wouldn't do to get the 'chop' out here," remarked Mike, echoing our thoughts and taking cover beside a huge fir tree. "Have you ever seen how much 'ammo' those 'Forts' carry? Absolute barrow loads!" he added.

"You're right," I said. "We once had a lost Fort land at Harwell when we on O.T.U. and the whole length of the fuselage was taken up with ammunition racks. They seemed to carry as much 'ammo' as bombs."

While we sheltered, awaiting the aerial battle to pass over we shared one of our rare cigarettes in a small celebration. It had been the first sign of life for some days and was welcome proof that the war was still being waged in our absence.

We presumed that the bombers were on their way to assist the American 9th Army, which according to our last reckoning was coming up from the South, though still some way off. As we continued our advance, we stopped from time to time, listening and feeling for the distant thud of falling bombs, but no sound came to give us any hope from that direction.

It was a lonely progress day by day, and we were glad of each other's company in a world almost devoid of human activity, so that when at last we saw a group of farm workers we almost felt like wishing them the time of day, but still keen to retain our treasured freedom our immediate reaction was to take cover.

It was late afternoon and watching from behind a convenient hedge we noted the slow but steady progress of the four distant figures as they bent and stretched on their way up the field. "They're planting something," said Mike.

"Of course they're planting something, you clot - ruddy potatoes! What do you expect at this time of year?" added Buzz witheringly.

"Yes, but how shall we know where they've planted them?" enquired Mike. "They could be anywhere, and we could do with some spuds now our turnips have nearly gone."

"If we can find two we can find all the rest," I announced confidently, remembering the toiling hours spent potato planting with my father before the war. "We just have to be patient and wait until they pack up and go home," I added. At last, the light was beginning to fade, the distant figures left the scene and collecting their bicycles from the far hedge rode off into the gathering dusk.

Unwilling to leave our cover until they were safely out of sight, we then crossed the wide expanse of field to the approximate area of operations and almost at once unearthed the first potato. Working systematically and searching at regular intervals we were soon able to collect as many as we could reasonably carry and happily left the scene assured of nourishment for at least the next few days.

Sheltering in a nearby wood for the night, we cleaned the earth from our winnings mostly by feel. It was almost dark and rubbing off the few eyes already shooting found that the potatoes though slightly woolly, still retained their flavour and were much easier to eat than the turnips which had been on the woody side.

Next morning at dawn, before the return of the workers to their labours we were on our way with the rising sun behind us, looking forward to another day.

The huge blocks of forest had now largely disappeared and we found ourselves with less dense cover, as open fields took their place and we descended from rolling hill country into a long flat valley of farms and distant cattle. "Now we shall have to watch out," said Buzz. "They'll be able to see us for miles if we're not careful."

"There are some roads down there too," I added. "Do you see the double row of trees running in straight lines and joining up with others?"

"Perhaps we ought to think about travelling by night," suggested Mike.

"And walk straight into a farmyard to be set upon by roaring dogs?" put in Buzz. "I'd rather take the risk by day. You can at least see the enemy in time to take some action."

I was inclined to agree and so we carried on, sometimes making vast detours to keep within the shadow of the hedgelines. The hedges were so unkempt - most of the farm workers now being in the forces - that we could not see through the undergrowth and therefore had to make frequent sallies through to the other side with great caution to inspect for any occupants in the adjoining field who would no doubt be suspicious of our presence. It was of necessity a lengthy process, particularly where ditches were involved, but the exercise enabled us to proceed in confidence without undue anxiety until the next change of course was required when the drill was repeated. Time was of no importance, but the fear of discovery was always with us, and having got so far we were becoming doubly cautious. It was while we were quietly negotiating an open field gate that a sudden apparition shook us rigid. A great fox, leaping up from under our feet, became suddenly airborne, to go shooting off across the field in great leaps and bounds. It was difficult to say who was the most shocked, ourselves or the fox, both of us being completely unaware of the other, such was our silent approach. Mike said it was as big as a wolf, and it was certainly the biggest fox that any of us had ever seen.

The incident though harmless in itself, brought home to us the hidden risks of our way of life, and we were thankful that it was only a fox and not the farmer's Alsatian.

As it was about midday we allowed ourselves the luxury of a rest and a bite to eat to steady our nerves, while leaning against the gate on look-out.

Crossing various farm tracks on which horses' hoof-prints appeared remarkably fresh as were the droppings, we decided to keep to the meadows rather than freshly cultivated ground where planting might be in progress.

Later on in the afternoon Buzz stopped suddenly and pointed, "Is that water over there? Look, you can see it shining between the trees!" We both stopped, and following his gaze agreed that it could be water glinting in the evening sun. "Perhaps it's a lake," I said, "in which case we'd better keep to the right of it. We don't want to have to walk all round it!" It was still some way off and it was evening before we discovered to our horror that it was not a lake, but a wide river, dashing any hope of further progress. Sitting on the bank considering our chances, we were quickly aware of a strange distant throbbing sound which we could not pin-point. On the few small roads we had crossed there had been no traffic and the nearest farm was a mile away.

As the sound grew perceptibly louder we prepared ourselves for a rush to cover, but were taken completely by surprise as an enormous barge swept round a bend in the river, proceeded by a massive bow wave.

Flinging ourselves flat to the ground, petrified, we watched the long low superstructure draw level and pass us, the loud throbbing of the diesels now plain. A plume of smoke hung in the air to mark its passage as the gathering wash rippled along under the bank. It was all over in a few minutes but we had time to note the helmsman leaning on the wheel to bring her round, though we were confident we had not been discovered.

We were unused to seeing such large vessels on inland water-ways even on the Thames, and Mike exclaimed, "Have you ever seen such a huge ship on a river? It was as long as a football pitch!"

"It looked very much like a small tanker," remarked Buzz, "but this is a very big river, certainly wide enough for two of those monsters to pass."

"The River Weser, deep and wide washes its banks on the southern side," I began to recite, remembering some long forgotten lines which seemed appropriate.

"The Weser. You don't think it's the river Weser do you?" asked Mike, as they both looked at me in alarm.

"I've no idea," I replied. "It could be, but what difference does it make? It's still too big to cross."

That night, ensconced in a small spinney not far from the river, we discussed our progress and various possibilities now that our advance was thwarted. Finishing the last of the bread, it was essential that we find a new food source before the potatoes ran out now that we were trapped by the river.

Casting our minds back to the last remembered news bulletin, we decided that it was entirely possible that we were now indeed sitting on the banks of the river Weser, and if that was so we could congratulate ourselves on our navigational skills.

But for the moment, thoughts centred on the possibility of finding a small boat somewhere along the river bank in which to make our escape to the other side. It was unlikely, but as the river was at least twice the width of the Thames at London Bridge we could not possibly attempt to swim it or float across on a log as the current was too swift. We knew that the river would have few bridges and those only in big towns, into which we dared not go.

Waking early to loud bird songs we set off up river planning to walk for half a day before returning to base for the night, and the next day to proceed down river in the opposite direction in the faint hope of finding some means of continuing our advance.

It was a beautiful spring day, and as we made rapid but silent progress through the dew drenched grass on the river bank, startled herons rose before us to flap lazily up river in slow measured flight. But there were little other signs of life apart from a few cattle which we tried not to startle, as they were evidently not used to the sight of humans and raised the their heads in unison at our approach to follow closely in a rather embarrassing fashion.

Our first instinct had been to wave our arms and rush at them, but we soon gave that up as they high-tailed it across the field, throwing up great clods of earth, so that anyone watching would have immediately known that something was afoot. We had to remind ourselves that we were not in England, where this activity might have gone unremarked in a much more heavily populated countryside.

At midday we stopped and rested. The river water was quite palatable, and we had a chew on a couple of potatoes apiece. Our stomachs having shrunk considerably, it did not take much to fill them, and we were soon on the return leg, timing ourselves by our one remaining watch - I had lost mine in the descent into Holland.

We had seen no signs of a boat, but then we did not really expect to find one. The natives, if any, had no need to cross the river, and probably rarely did so.

We had to be constantly on the alert for the river transport and two more immense barges had passed us during our short time on the river bank, but now that we knew what to expect we had ample time to take cover. It was evident that the Germans were making full use of this North-South artery which was virtually impervious to attack except where occasional bridges crossed the river.

Towards evening the wind increased, veering round to the West, bringing with it exciting sounds of aerial activity coupled with the thud of muffled explosions. Could this mark the present position of the no doubt very fluid front line, or was it an attempt to knock out the opposition in readiness for a further advance?

We had no means of knowing, but had by now convinced ourselves that if the speed of advance had been maintained from its earlier known position, the British 2nd Army was now not far away.

That night, back in our hide-out, our long awaited hopes began to materialise. The Western sky was aglow in palest light. Scarcely able to believe our eyes. we watched the distant horizon, fascinated by the vague tremors reflected on the high cloud, and the intermittent glow of imagined gunfire. Voicing our thoughts and experiences of bombing operations, Mike said, "That's not a target area, the whole affair's not red enough. And there are no searchlights." We both agreed and Buzz remarked, "There's no flak either, but would we see flak from that distance? We don't know how far away it is."

"Well, we know that flak and searchlights can be seen for over twenty miles on a clear night," I added.

"Yes, but that's from the air," put in Mike, "and we're on the ground."

The conversation lapsed, awaiting further proof of these exciting developments, but we spent a large part of the night studying the distant horizon watching for any change in the illuminations which did not diminish but rather, increased. Or was it our imagination?

Chapter 11

Woken early in the morning by strange repetitive rasping sounds, Mike crept out of our small spinney to investigate. He soon returned with a smile on his face.

"Ruddy herd of cows on the edge of the wood," he announced, and amused and relieved we at once recognised country sounds at their face value, being ever suspicious of every unusual noise from whatever quarter.

Following a brief breakfast and a drink from the river we set off down-stream still on the lookout for a boat. In the warm sunshine our great coats were becoming a burden, but lumbered as we were with our few treasured possessions we preferred to wear them rather than carry them. The nights were still cold, and they had become part of our life.

We walked all day, crossing small streams and ditches and forcing our way through thick undergrowth where woods came down to the river bank, the only sign of life the occasional river barge.

Towards evening we came upon a huge barn set back from the river, and having reluctantly given up any hope of continuing our advance, decided to make this our base pending the arrival of our troops which we felt was imminent. The barn had two floors with a ladder up to the loft, and on the ground floor were the visible signs of over-wintered cattle with the accompanying troughs and hay-racks still in position. In one corner was a pile of old turnips which might come in useful should our stay be prolonged.

This seemed the ideal hide-out and climbing the rickety ladder we were delighted to find the loft two feet deep in hay. It was all very comfortable compared with many of our previous resting places, and we were prepared to sit it out for a week or more if necessary. We had seen nobody for days and now that the cattle had gone to the fields the barn was no longer in regular use.

We were probably more cheerful than we had been for the whole of our journey, feeling very relaxed, luxuriating on our soft bed of hay discussing the now distinct possibility of a happy end to our exertions. We fell to wondering where our fellow members on the original march had finished up and whether they were now as many miles East as we were West, and how many others had seized the opportunity of escaping from the marching column and how they had fared.

And then Buzz raised a point which caused us to rethink our position. "I suppose you realise," he said, "that this barn will be one of the first landmarks that our tanks and gunners will take out!"

"You mean they might think it could be used as an observation point by the enemy," I answered.

"Yes," he replied, "because it's probably the only high point for miles around in this flat valley." This distinct possibility was a cause for some concern, and then Mike added, "Whatever happens, we could very well finish up in the thick of it when the time comes. They might even send in a Typhoon to take it out!"

We had nearly made it, and the thought of having come so far to be wiped out by our own troops was a sobering thought. We decided to lie low and wait events and if necessary vacate the barn and return to open country where we might feet safer. We considered it unlikely that this quiet backwater would be the scene of a major operation in river crossing, and that it was more likely that the town with bridges would take the brunt of the attack.

As night fell, it became clear that we had not imagined the shimmering glow of the previous evening. From our vantage point the western horizon came suddenly to life in the gathering darkness, the distant rise and fall of flickering light boring into our eyes. Faintly, carried on the wind came the short sharp note of gunfire as distinct from the thud of bombs and we knew it would not be long.

We slept well that night on our bed of hay, and early next morning scoured the local countryside for anything faintly edible as a change from our stable diet of potatoes, but with little luck. We had now entered into a confident routine of resting from our labours, alert yet relaxed. We could do no more but just wait patiently for something to happen.

Early in the afternoon something happened which was to freeze our blood. We had been talking quietly, when as with a sixth sense all conversation suddenly ceased; in absolute silence, ears cocked, the distant sound returned to stun the brain - "Jerries!"

Leaping up, we rushed to the side of the barn to peer between the riven timbers. German soldiers, fully equipped with all sorts of battle-gear were entering the field.

There was no escape. Any attempt to leave the cover of the barn would be seen and we knew that any running figure was liable to bring out the worst in the enemy. We were trapped by this least expected invasion of our privacy, but it proved to us beyond a shadow of doubt that the British 2nd Army was not far off.

There was nothing for it, and after a hurried consultation we decided to bury ourselves under the hay and hope for the best.

All that afternoon, from the depths of the hay, we listened to the clinking of tools as the Jerries dug themselves in around the curve of the river bank. We had no idea of the passage of time, or light and dark, but listening to the sounds of heavy boots on the creaking ladder, we realised that the hay loft was suddenly full of German soldiers coming off duty. The muffled voices and heavy thuds as they flung off their webbing penetrated our dusty world, and nerves jangling we waited for the discovery that did not come.

Finally, all movement ceased and we presumed that the soldiers had settled down for the night as the weight above us was now considerable. The sudden alarm and fear we had at first experienced had long since departed, and now that we were in the hands of fate a strange composure had overtaken us, calming our shattered nerves.

Conversation was impossible, and trying desperately not to cough or sneeze we attempted to sleep, but sleep might bring on the risk of snoring, and silence was essential. We need not have bothered as those above us filled the barn with grunts and noisy expulsions of wind throughout the night. We slept little, waiting only for the long night to be over, to be relieved of the incessant weight bearing down upon us.

Anxiety returned as with loud shouts and heavy movements the throng above us gathered their kit together and descended the ladder to the floor below. After a few minutes, silence reigned, as voices trailed off into the distance and muffled sounds of activity along the river bank recommenced. "I think they've all gone!" I whispered to Buzz who was lying next to me. "I'm going to have a look," and carefully raising my head to peer through the layers of hay, discovered that we were at last alone.

Rising silently from my hidden bed, I advanced to the top of the ladder and looked down. Below me sat a German major and two other officers seated at a small table covered with maps. Unknown to us, the barn had become headquarters for a regiment of Marines making a last stand at the river.

Beating a hasty but silent retreat, I returned to my lair under the hay and told the others what I had seen.

Shortly afterwards, a Jerry soldier returning to the loft, perhaps to retrieve something he had left behind, missed his footing and fell down in the hole between Buzz and myself, thus exposing both of us to his startled gaze. "Gott in Himmel!" he exclaimed, his face visibly blanching as he hastily recoiled and recovered his balance to stand over us in a somewhat threatening manner.

We were at a disadvantage, but at our sudden appearance he was probably more shocked than we were and in an immediate attempt to treat the whole affair as a joke we started laughing as a relief from the build up of tension, which, under the circumstances was probably the best thing we could have done. With an uncertain smile, the soldier's face brightened, and smiling broadly he began to see the humour of the occasion.

Our final denouement had been no great shock to us, we had been expecting it since the evening before, and to be honest we were relieved that the tension was over, though of course still uncertain of our future.

Rising stiffly from the wisps of hay we accompanied him down the ladder to stand before the German officers proclaiming ourselves 'Kriegsgefangenen', so that no doubt could arise as to our status.

Introducing us, the German soldier with some amusement, explained our presence, whereupon the officers fortunately responded in similar fashion, and after considerable discussion among themselves took our word that we were British P.O.W.s.

It was lucky that the senior officer was well versed in the rights of prisoners and even more fortunate that he was a member of a Marine regiment and not an SS regiment when things might have been very different.

Having been finally accepted for what we were, we marked the occasion by handing round our few English cigarettes which were accepted with alacrity.

Discussing how lucky we were to have been recaptured by regular soldiers, we decided that the future looked reasonably bright as we were marched off with a platoon of soldiers to a farm some distance away. The only sour note was that they lumbered each of us with a large black box of machine gun ammunition which we were forced to carry with some difficulty, but that was only a reflection of the German mentality to prove that they were still the masters. Upon leaving the barn field, a quick glance round soon accounted for the sounds of activity which had earlier filtered through to our hiding place. Dispersed along the river bank, well dug in, were the guns and equipment of a well organised force. Somehow we hoped our captors would survive the battle to come.

On our arrival at the farm, which obviously contained the cookhouse facilities, we were to receive our first real food since we had escaped, and we sat in the sun in the farmyard feeling moderately cheerful. Mike, holding aloft a precious sausage and extolling the virtues of our first frankfurter, shouted in sudden fury, as in the wink of an eye the prize was plucked from his outstretched hand. Like lightning, a cockerel scratching about nearby, had leapt into the air and with remarkable agility snatched the offered tidbit to race off across the farmyard at high speed, leaving Mike empty handed. The Jerries seated nearby laughed like drains at his obvious displeasure, and we realised that we ourselves had not had the occasion to laugh aloud for ages.

A little later, two Jerries, who had been detailed to commandeer a horse and wagon from the farmer, gestured to us to jump up and we climbed into the long blue high-sided cart, which as Buzz remarked with some irony, looked remarkably like a coffin.

With one Jerry leaning up against the front of the cart whipping up the horse, we set off, to where we knew not. The second Jerry was posted as 'look-out' at the rear of the wagon, though we did not immediately appreciate the significance of this precaution. In this distinctly uncomfortable vehicle we were to travel most of the day, but it was marginally better that walking.

Rattling along, we relived our recent hair raising experience, and decided that perhaps after all our discovery had been imminent and unavoidable anyhow, as we could not possibly have remained in that prostrate position for an unlimited period. As it was, we calculated that we had been under the hay for some sixteen hours and our throats were still raw from inhaling the dust.

"Did you see the fright on that Jerries' face when he fell down the hole between us?" recalled Mike, "looked as if he was going to pass out!"

"His face went as white as a sheet," added Buzz. "I thought we'd had it for a moment."

"I must say I half expected a bayonet or a boot when his fear turned to anger," I remarked. "That was a good wheeze to try and turn the whole affair into a great joke," said Buzz. "Probably saved our lives."

Congratulating ourselves on the outcome of a situation which could easily have gone the other way, we sat back against the sides of the wagon and enjoyed the dappled sunlight as we passed along tree lined tracks and minor roads.

We were soon to come upon the undoubted results of low-level attack by the R.A.F. as serried rows of trees stood starkly at half-mast, some decapitated, others hanging down, the ends of the broken branches touching the ground.

It was strange that we had heard nothing of this while on our earlier travels, but concluded that we had probably been many miles North, when we had first arrived at the river, and therefore the attack had been out of earshot.

As we progressed, more immediate signs of the war appeared in the shape of broken wagons, of long-dead horses, their bloated bodies huge, their entrails in hideous view. It was plain that the enemy, now desperately short of fuel, was reduced to using horse transport to assist in the war effort, as here and there under the roadside trees were upended rifles stuck in the ground supporting the tin helmets of those once engaged in bringing up supplies. It was the first time we had witnessed the effects of war on the ground at close quarters and it was a chilling prospect to us as aircrew, who had always been far removed from the results of our endeavours, though we had suffered in the process. From our point of view, our efforts had been at last worthwhile, in that the German war machine was slowly grinding to a halt, now that the cumulative effect of the R.A.F. bombing raids was becoming apparent.

We had hardly left the macabre scene when a sudden shout of "Achtung - Achtung!" from the Jerry at the rear of the wagon galvanised the driver into furious action. Whipping up his horse he swung the wagon into the shelter of the trees. Quickly unharnessing the horse, and driving it into the woods, the Jerries motioned us to take cover in the roadside ditch behind a pile of stones, and only just in time. Unseen by us, a flight of R.A.F. Typhoons appeared from nowhere and at ground level howled along beside the trees.

It was a magnificent sight, the Typhoons in their invasion livery of broad white stripes, and so enthralled were we that we became totally unaware of the dangers.

Shortly they returned in earnest, all guns firing to shoot up the road ahead of us. Odd bullets whined and ricocheted off the road, sending up sudden spurts of dust and the sound of cannon shells splintering nearby trees added to the rising crescendo.

For a few minutes, all was confusion, but as quickly as the Typhoons had appeared, they disappeared from sight and sound and peace returned.

Now that it was over, we found our captors convulsed with laughter at the thought of British P.O.W.s being at the receiving end of their compatriots' guns. They were highly amused at the irony of the situation and we happily joined in secure in the knowledge that we were soon to be the victors.

Capturing the startled horse with difficulty and putting him back in the shafts, our captors resumed their position fore and aft and we clambered back into the wagon to continue our journey.

It was not long before we were to appreciate just what had been the attraction for the ever searching Typhoons. Around the bend was the magnet that had drawn their fire with such vigour. On both sides of the road, drawn up under the broken trees, stood the shattered remnants of a Panzer regiment on its way up to the front.

Amid the suffocating smoke from several blazing lorries were light tanks and troop carriers parked so close together that they were in immediate danger of being drawn into the conflagration. It had obviously been a panic dispersal without any thought of extricating undamaged vehicles before they too caught fire and looking at the occupants, it was evident that most of them had not long left school.

They were perhaps fourteen or fifteen years old, no doubt belonging to the Hitler Youth and suddenly drawn into battle. This was their first baptism of fire. Their white, shocked faces stark against the black uniforms emblazoned with swastikas, we felt momentarily acutely sorry for them, but they were part of the enemy war machine and had been trained for this purpose from an early age.

Our captors made no comment as we hastened through the broken ranks, no doubt hardened by the sight around them and we were soon out into unspoilt country once more, while marvelling at the freedom of the air the R.A.F. now enjoyed. It seemed a far cry from the days when a fleet of Lancs or Halibags might immediately bring up a squadron of night fighters. Mike, chewing on a hunk of bread saved from breakfast in the farmyard, declared that it was lunchtime, and Buzz and I, rummaging in our bags, retrieved similar gut filling morsels, while conversation centred on the interesting part we had just played in getting mixed up in a minor battle in which we were unable physically, to take part.

Later in the day there were further signs of aircraft activity, and it was not long before we passed through a small town teeming with German soldiers, and like a wasp nest disturbed, the atmosphere was tense.

No doubt a potential pocket of resistance, it had received a considerable battering and as we passed through the central square, I am not ashamed to say that we kept our heads down, not wishing to be strung up as 'Terrorfliegers'.

There were no signs of bombs and we had heard nothing to denote this, but many roofs displayed the crisscross of bare battens where large areas of tiles had disappeared and roof guttering hung down limply at all angles around the shattered windows. Outside the hostelry stood a huge brewer's dray from which the valuable horses had obviously been removed, and arching streams of beer still spouted spasmodically from the punctured barrels, where stray bullets had found their mark.

It was a scene of some destruction and we were glad that our captors did not hesitate but passed straight on through, intent only in carrying out their orders, which any good German soldier would inevitably do.

At the end of a tiring but invigorating trip, we came to our final destination, a small camp festooned with the usual barbed wire and 'goon'-boxes, but where we were to be virtually our own masters.

Jerry guards were still in attendance, but they did not bother us and we did not bother them.

Everyone seemed to be waiting for something to happen and the atmosphere between captors and captives became almost friendly in the last days.

The inmates were composed of all nationalities and all branches of the services, some being recently captured and full of their latest exploits. It was an interesting and exciting time. The question of food being uppermost in our mind, we at once broke into the German food stores and came away with all manner of exciting tins, one of which contained the most beautiful corned beef imaginable. But a diet of corned beef played havoc with our insides, now incapable of digesting anything other than roughage, and all three of us, amongst others, became very ill indeed, so ill in fact that death might seem a happy release from a hugely distended stomach which would not subside.

Relief came at last with repeated trips to the latrines which rapidly became the popular meeting place for inmates to discuss their symptoms.

Leaving all forms of meat severely alone, we then progressed to macaroni which at once soothed the gut and restored a lining to the stomach.

While recovering from this digestive set back, Mike and Buzz, in the company of others, reclined peacefully in the sun while I hunted through my treasured pack which had been part of me for over a thousand miles, and took out my drawing book in an attempt to record those exciting days of freedom which had become indelibly printed on my mind. I still had a stump of pencil left which was fortunate as there was absolutely nothing in the camp, except, entirely due to our own efforts, a little more variety of food with which we now rationed ourselves most carefully, having learnt our lesson.

After a few days, a lone R.A.F. Auster spotter plane appeared in the distance and overflew the camp at low level to be hailed with a sea of waving arms and loud cheers from the delirious inmates. There was no sign of opposition from the goon-boxes as he circled the camp rocking his wings to show that he had marked our position.

And then at last, all along the western horizon, black palls of smoke suddenly appeared heralding the advance of our troops as they knocked out small pockets of resistance in their rapid advance.

The next day was the day none of us will ever forget. We were no longer P.O.W.s. For us the war was over!

The first British tanks appeared at about midday, approaching at speed across the fields from all directions to go shooting past the camp in pursuit of the invisible enemy. It was an awe inspiring occasion, as with roaring engines and clattering tracks they swept past, leaving a trail of wind-blown dust in their wake.

So great was the excitement that soon the roofs of the huts were dressed overall with waving figures unable to contain themselves, and as could be imagined the Frenchmen among us were quickly reduced to tears, such was the emotion generated.

It was not long before one overloaded roof unable to sustain its burden, suddenly collapsed to disappear in a cloud of choking dust, but those affected clambered from the wreckage still wreathed in smiles. Fortunately no one was injured and they quickly regained a vantage point on another roof to the resounding cheers of their comrades.

While most of the tanks thundered past, two stopped and the occupants jumped down for a chat with those hanging like monkeys on the main gate, whereupon one of the 'brown jobs' in the camp, a recent P.O.W., proclaimed them to be part of the 7th Armoured Division, as he was one of the few to recognise the insignia on the tanks.

Towards evening a lorry swept up to the gates to deliver a load of English bread which was eagerly passed around to form the basis of a safer diet. Meanwhile the Jerry guards were walking listlessly around, looking rather forlorn. The boot was on the other foot and now they had an uncertain future.

Taking advantage of the general atmosphere, I walked up to the nearest Jerry and promptly relieved him of his bayonet. Acknowledging the reversal of fortunes, he made no attempt to resist my claim. The bayonet now rests in my fireplace, serving a more useful purpose than the one for which it was designed.

Some few days later, a fleet of lorries arrived to carry us to Detmold, a large airbase some fifty miles south where we were to board R.A.F. transport planes bound for England. Our incarceration in a foreign land was over, and rather like going on extended leave, we boarded the waiting Douglas Dakotas in high spirits as if we were going on holiday. There were no seats on these transport aircraft so we just all sat on the floor, about fifty of us, conversation hushed, waiting for the roar of the engines. But to be honest, as soon as the engines started many of us were overtaken by an attack of nerves. The last time we had had been airborne had been our last, and to add to our discomfort we were not equipped with parachutes.

Listening to the steady roar of the engines, confidence returned, and we duly landed at Brize Norton to a heroes' return, which was unexpected and very moving.

As the Dakota taxied up to the huge flag-festooned hanger, we clambered out, an ill-assorted collection of untidy individuals, to be welcomed and escorted each by a W.A.A.F. to small tables in the hanger where tea and cakes were served.

It was very civilised, though the effect upon some of the older time-served Kriegies was evident. Some of them had not seen, let alone touched a woman for many years and tended to shy away like startled horses at the first contact and had to be coaxed along like small boys going to school.

It was amusing yet understandable in the sudden transition to an England and freedom they had left so long ago. Some of them had lived out almost the whole of the war in a strange limbo and it would take time and care before they could return to normality, if they ever could.

Later, we were to luxuriate in hot baths, and in a well planned operation passed through the disinfection chambers where all manner of strange chemicals were sprayed upon our tingling torsos to remove the possibility of foreign bodies.

The following medical inspection concluded our rehabilitation and we were then measured and weighed. I had lost over three stone while a P.O.W. and some were in worse condition.

Queueing up to be issued with a whole new set of kit, Mike remarked that we had actually arrived home before the end of the war and I was able to say that it was a year to the day when I was shot down, 27th April 1944.

The official end to the war in Europe was not to be until 8th May 1945, and strangely enough it was on Luneburg Heath, the scene of our escape, where the German surrender was signed.

In 'best blue' we proudly went on leave, cheered by the thought of double rations for three months.

It was great to be on home ground again, to be welcomed by the station master at our local station who had known me from boyhood, and others, alighting from the train, who were obviously delighted to see me again.

I later learned that somehow my mother always knew that I would come home, though many thousands did not, and it is to them that this book is dedicated.

EPILOGUE

My fellow crew member, Rebel, the mid-upper gunner, and the only other survivor from the aircraft, was not one of our escape party, and therefore, unfortunately, I lost contact with him upon repatriation. No doubt he was soon sent home to his native Canada.

I was to learn that Eleanor was already married when I arrived home, and although this was naturally a cause of some regret, the news did not floor me. That part of my life was over, and such was the delight of being free, and home amongst my family and friends, that its significance soon faded.

Buzz and Mike have sadly disappeared into the dim distance over the years, but I hope that they may read this book, and be reminded of the exciting times we shared together.

I was fortunate, in that all my friends and relatives returned safely from the war, my two school friends from the Navy and John Winship who had so enjoyed his time on 'Spits'. My cousin Haddon had gone in with the tanks at Anzio, and suffered considerable deafness as a result of the din of battle, and remains partially deaf to this day, an affliction partly alleviated by a disability pension, a cause of some amusement to the rest of us, not unmixed with envy!

My brother Dick was recalled from his long range though not unexciting duties in Ferry Command prior to the invasion, when everyone was pressed into service. As I had surmised, he was involved in the great airborne armada towing in gliders, on D Day, at the Arnhem show, and again at the Rhine crossing among others, where he received a baptism of 'flak' which very fortunately only put him into hospital for a short time, to have the bits removed.

The heavy losses inflicted on Bomber Command during the period of which I write, were of course due to the obvious results of total war, but two contributing factors stand out which were not appreciated at the time. H2S, a clever adaptation of science, which was able to reflect images on the ground onto a screen in the aircraft and thus assist in accurate navigation and target identification, was also being picked up by enemy fighters on their radar screens, enabling them to 'home' onto a particular bomber with great accuracy. Later, as awareness of this dreadful fact became apparent, the general use of H2S was much reduced and confined mainly to target areas.

Perhaps an even more serious factor was the 'blind spot', that area under the belly of all our wartime bombers which was totally at the mercy of enemy fighters, attacking unseen from below. Alas, our anti-fighter radar did not cover this vulnerable area.

There is no doubt that the Germans were very clever and were quick to design deadly new weapons for their twin-engined fighters in order to take advantage of this weak spot. Basically the idea was simple but ingenious. Twin cannon were fixed in an upward firing position at the rear of the cockpit, to be loaded and cocked by the navigator/radar operator, but these were actually fired by the pilot in the front seat, by means of a special harmonised sight. Using this method, their fighters were able to make a leisurely, safe approach from below the bomber, unseen by the gunners, and fire a quick accurate burst of incendiary cannon-fire into our wing fuel tanks, close to the engines, before rapidly breaking away to escape the almost inevitable maelstrom above them.

This must, by any standards, be considered a somewhat cowardly action, but the enemy was desperate. Little skill and little danger were involved in this manoeuvre, and many night-fighter pilots, shooting from a level platform were able to claim five, and sometimes as many as ten, certain 'kills' in one night's operation during which they would land, refuel and re-arm to return to the attack.

This system was without doubt the cause of our heaviest losses, particularly on moonlit nights, but despite this, our bombers were never fitted with any means of defence to counteract the danger to this 'blind spot'. There had been attempts earlier in the war to fit lower gun turrets, but the 'powers that be' at the time believed that these might rarely be used, and so they were not fitted. How wrong they were. Whoever denied us this essential protection had a lot to answer for, because even with our .303 pea-shooters, we could have effectively joined battle at close range with a fighter 'cruising' immediately below, momentarily flying in formation with us.

Today, 50 years on, I took back with a certain pride, glad to have been involved, though saddened for those not given a 'time of return'. I have tried over the intervening years to discover from various R.A.F. sources just what happened to the remainder of my crew, with little success as to their actual burial place, until a remarkable twist of fate completed my search.

My son-in-law Steve, at this time flying Harriers in the R.A.F., happened to pass on to me a copy of 'Air Mail', the R.A.F. Association's journal, the first I had seen for probably 40 years. In this journal, there is a section for persons seeking information about relatives and friends lost in the war, and to my amazement the name John McGlynn leapt from the page. Killed in action, I knew he must have been our rear-gunner, as the place and date given proved without doubt. I immediately wrote to the address given, expecting to hear from some relative, but was fascinated to discover the inquiry came not from a relative, but from a young couple, Jane Pears and Frank Allen, who, being greatly interested in the war years, had discovered his grave in a Maastricht cemetery.

Quite by chance, Jane had photographed the stone carved with his name, being greatly touched by the fact that he was the youngest there. Jane has since, with great patience and research, discovered a family tree of relatives, some of whom also had little idea as to what had happened to him, apart from the fact that he was certified killed in action, as were the rest of my friends.

So at last I know that the five remaining members of my crew rest in a foreign land, in the cemetery in Maastricht, where their graves are deservedly honoured by the Dutch people.